BOOK 5 OF THE WITCHBOUND SAGA

the VEILED THREAT of MAGIC

NATALIE GIBSON

Livonia, Michigan

THE VEILED THREAT OF MAGIC
Copyright © 2022 Natalie Gibson

All rights reserved. No part of this publication may be reproduced, distributed, or transmitted in any form or by any means, including photocopying, recording, or other electronic or mechanical methods, without the prior written permission of the publisher, except in the case of brief quotations embodied in critical reviews and certain other noncommercial uses permitted by copyright law. For permission requests, please write to the publisher.

This book is a work of fiction. The characters, incidents, and dialogue are drawn from the author's imagination and are not to be construed as real. Any resemblance to actual events or persons, living or dead, is entirely coincidental.

Published by BHC Press

Library of Congress Control Number: 2021944527

ISBN Numbers:
978-1-64397-325-8 (Hardcover)
978-1-64397-326-5 (Softcover)
978-1-64397-327-2 (Ebook)

For information, write:
BHC Press
885 Penniman #5505
Plymouth, MI 48170

Visit the publisher:
www.bhcpress.com

ALSO BY
NATALIE GIBSON

Witchbound
For the Love of Magic
The Dying Art of Magic
The Magic Number
The Nature of Magic

Multi-author Anthologies
In Creeps the Night
A Winter's Romance

To anyone who's ever been fooled by a pretty face
and a washboard stomach… Don't sweat it.
It happens to the best of us.

THE VEILED THREAT OF MAGIC

ONE

Christy Adams couldn't sleep. She wouldn't. The hands were waiting for her there in her nightmares. So many uninvited hands on her body. Some pawed at her, tore at her clothes, caressed her skin as they exposed it. Some were balled into fists that bruised and split her hide. None of them cared for her, for what *she* wanted and needed. No, she couldn't sleep anymore tonight. She had given those hands too much of her real life. They couldn't have her dreams too. It was only a few hours until sunrise anyway.

Christy walked the grounds in only her thin satiny pink nightgown that barely covered her panties. Her only adornment, a modified medic-alert button on a necklace. It was a warm night. Everyone but the Nephilim guards were in bed. Nathalia had made them swear not to touch Christy, and the ancient-winged Guardians gave her a wide birth. She could do nothing to entice them. Not that she hadn't tried. A Nephilim mate would secure her place in this world and that was something Christy desperately wanted. She felt adrift, floating along, living half a life, never belonging, always apart.

Ever grateful to the Daughters of Women, Christy couldn't complain. She could, but she shouldn't. Wouldn't. Living with them was a bizarre blessing. She walked past a row of state-of-the-art solar panels and then a crumbling well house from when it had been an operating Spanish mission. The dichotomy wasn't lost on Christy. This place the Austin Daughters called home was a perfect reflection of the Daughters themselves. They were as modern as possible. Some of the technology they implemented in their everyday lives wasn't even available to the public, yet the old ways were still there. Whether they admitted it or not, this was a religion and like all religions there was a hierarchy. There were leaders and followers and then there was Christy.

She didn't think she was going any particular place as she thought about all this, just a stroll to ease her mind. She let her feet take whatever path they were drawn to. One in front of the other, she barely registered that she had drifted far from the main buildings, so close to the shield's edge. Her shield. It hummed in response to her nearness. She could sense it even when she couldn't see it, even when no one could see it. Christy stood with the moonlight reflecting off her blond hair, giving it a ghostly white quality, and looked at the grandeur of her magic. She still had trouble believing it was her doing.

She heard a rustling in the bushes but managed to keep herself from jumping. She stared at the place just beyond. There were plenty of shadows there on the other side, plenty of places to hide. Whatever was there couldn't get through her shield. If not a bullet nor a knife-toting man could penetrate, neither could an animal. She was perfectly safe.

That was what she tried to tell herself when the giant monster stepped into view. It lumbered toward her. When it hit her shield, it was shocked to find it could not pass. It roared its frustration. Christy's shriek cut through the night silence. She pushed her panic button frantically.

There was no shortage of Nephilim on the Daughters of Women compound, and scarcely a second passed before five Nephilim landed around Christy. The monster didn't like that, and it growled. The Guardians heard it but they looked to her for guidance. "Where?" one of them barked. Eiran and Nathalia appeared shortly after. Nathalia embraced Christy and spoke inside her mind, *Sorry we are late. We went to your bedroom but you weren't there. What's happened?*

Christy was still shaking but pointed to the shield, right at the monster. She looked at them and then back at the behemoth. It was in plain sight, barely a yard away. A flap of wings and the Guardians were gone. They went to chase something they couldn't see.

Nathalia held her at arm's length. *Are you all right?*

Christy nodded.

Stay here. If there's something out there trying to get in, we will find it. Nathalia and Eiran didn't fly away, they simply disappeared. She and the beast were alone again.

Christy had never been this close to an Akhkharu—a Nephilim that had given in to their hunger beast and feasted on the flesh and blood of another Nephilim. That feast satisfied their terrible gnawing hunger but came at a great cost. They were slowly consumed by their beast until no more of their goodness remained. They could no longer stand the light of Ud, the sun, and Kiyahwe rejected them from her earthly protection from that light. Akhkharu were every bit as powerful as the Nephilim they once were and had none of the hindering morality.

Christy looked at the way it hovered a foot above the ground and she felt sure that this was an Akhkharu. It was as large as any Nephilim, more than seven feet tall and bulky. Its complexion could only be described as ruddy, dark and reddened even in the dim light of the bluing moon. Large, bat-like wings, tattered and torn, at least twelve feett in wingspan, extended from behind its shoulders. Its face was that of a man but one that might belong to a wild man. It was unkempt, unshaven, and uncared for. Its teeth were stained and sharp, and Christy had to force herself to stop imagining them tearing into her. Most disturbing were its eyes. Totally red, lid to lid and corner to corner, no pupil or iris, they were completely alien with their slight glow.

Then it spoke, "You are the shield maker." Her fear was replaced with wonder. His voice was a more extreme version of all the Nephilim's she'd heard. There were at least two voices coming from that one mouth and one of them, the most prominent, wasn't human. It sounded like a lion talking through its roar. Deep, the rumble resonated inside her and ignited the kindling she kept piled up in her heart. If she were honest with herself, the fire was a bit lower in her body than her heart.

Her knees felt weak, and she didn't trust herself to speak. She nodded instead. She was attracted to this monster for some reason, but she kept her hand wrapped loosely around the necklace she wore at night. It was like the ones old ladies used to get help when they fell and couldn't get up. It's what she used to alert the Nephilim guard if they were under attack. They hadn't seen him the first time, but she hadn't told them she could see something they couldn't. She knew an Akhkharu couldn't be trusted, this one more than most because of the attraction she felt toward it. Just in case, she threw a little extra layer on the shield for him specifically. Her shield didn't let anyone in she didn't want.

"You are mine." He said it almost as a question, in amazement, like he couldn't believe his own words. His red eyes burned a trail along her body, and she shuddered despite the warm air. "Your mother had this ability also?" He looked up at her shield as if he could sense it too.

Christy shook her head.

"Your maternal grandmother?" he asked in a voice that Christy imagined a cement truck filled with gravel would have.

Again she gave him the negative sign.

"You have had no training? And you accomplished this?" He gestured to the invisible but massive shield. He was clearly amazed.

Christy found her voice. "Some men came here with guns. They threatened me and the ones I care for. It just sprang up."

The monster growled. The sound should have scared her, but it did something completely unexpected. That sound comforted her.

"The Daughters don't have any shield makers. They don't even have any records of any others."

"No, there wouldn't be. I thought our mother's line had died out long ago. I am the only one left, as far as I know." His voices dropped and he said in an almost-seductive tone, "I can teach you."

"Christy, who are you talking to?"

She jumped. The world outside of the monster in front of her had faded away and a Nephilim had walked up beside her. She exhaled slowly.

"Christy," the monster rumbled, rolling the name around in his mouth like one might with a wine at a tasting. She liked the way he said it.

When she didn't answer his question, the Nephilim, whose name she thought was Jon, suggested that she go inside. "There is nothing out tonight. I don't know what frightened you, but we are not under attack," Jon informed her. "Is the shield compromised?" he asked, his eyebrows raised, his eyes opal white and sparkling in the low light.

"No, no. It's fine. I just had a nightmare and came out for a walk." It was the truth, and the Nephilim had a way of making everyone want to tell them the truth, so she didn't fight it. She didn't want to go in, but she couldn't think of a reasonable excuse to stay so Jon herded her away. She looked over her shoulder in as nonchalant a way as she could manage. The Akhkharu was there, watching her. She knew he would be waiting for her to come back, and she would, as soon as she could.

CHRISTY HAD a job to do that morning, but her mind wandered back to the events of the night. Was she going crazy? No one had seen the Akhkharu but her. How was that possible? She knew it wouldn't be there in the daytime, but she felt her eyes drifting that direction all morning. She looked to all the world like she was staring off into space, but she wasn't daydreaming. She was focused on that spot just beyond her shield where she imagined she could feel that monster looking at her hungrily. The way it said her name…

"We could move into the sun, if you feel a chill without Ud's light."

She tore her attention away from the sensational memory and looked at Sam. "Huh?"

"Your skin is bumpy, your body hair bristled. I have been told that is how the human body shows it is cold." Sam was a Nephilim, but not just any one. He was the Guardian of the One. Genevieve, the toddler playing between them, would be his Sinnis and, once endowed with her full power, would save the world. Sam was odd, as all the half-breeds were, but he was nicer to her than the others. At least he spoke to her in a friendly way. She knew he felt they were allies, both protectors of Genevieve.

"Oh, yes, thank you. I hadn't noticed how cool the shadows had gotten."

Christy stood, dusting the dirt and grass off her frayed jean shorts, and stepped out of the shade. She held her hands out to Genevieve and Juliet, the other toddler it was her duty to look after part of every day, and said, "Come on. Come here. Walk like big girls. Show me who's fastest." The girls giggled and toddled toward her, happy with the impromptu race. When it looked like Genevieve would win and Juliet knew it, Christy zig-zagged away and the game started anew. She turned and pretended to fall in just the right place for both girls to pounce on her simultaneously.

They rolled and tickled until Genevieve turned her attention to Sam. She ran after the giant as best she could, and he let her catch him. Sam didn't like Juliet for some reason so Christy gave her some extra affection while the other two played. The Nephilim all loved their prophesies and there was one about two daughters, one fair haired and one dark, who would betray and be betrayed and the One would be banished from her time. No one really knew what it meant and Jolie, Juliet's mom and the seer of the Daughters, said that hers was a difficult discipline. The future was always changing and prophesies were easily misinterpreted.

Juliet and Genevieve were close in age, born only days apart, and had for some time looked similar enough to be sisters. Then Genevieve had lost her dark hair all at once and it was replaced by golden. Maeve, Genevieve's mother and Abbess to the Daughters, had freaked. Her dad, Aaron, had said the same thing had happened to him. Sam never talked about it, but Christy knew he thought that particular prophesy was about Juliet and Genevieve and now they both looked the part.

Christy. Nathalia called to her, from goddess knows how far away. She'd had to go out on official Sinnis business this morning. *Christy.* She called again. She was giving Christy enough time to stop what she was doing and pay attention. Christy pointed out a small flower to Juliet to distract her so she could do what Nathalia demanded. Juliet squatted in that way only babies can and studied the small purple bud. *There is a new Nephilim coming. Please allow him to pass through. Tell anyone who questions his presence that I was the one who allowed it.*

Genevieve, interested in what had Juliet so enthralled, came over to investigate. Rather than share the discovery with her friend, Juliet grabbed the flower, plucked it, and held it pressed against her chest. She turned her shoulders to keep Genevieve from seeing. When Genevieve started crying, Juliet recanted and tried to give the flower to her. The fact that it was crumpled only made Genevieve cry harder.

Christy couldn't answer Nathalia back. The magic didn't work that way. Nathalia could only broadcast her own thoughts and feelings into others. She couldn't hear the workings of other people's minds. Christy stood and focused on the shield. Nathalia couldn't tell her this new Nephilim's name, but she had broadcasted a faint image that Christy could use.

INI-HERIT BELIAL Maru's feet came to rest on the cool, well-maintained grass of the Daughters of Women's courtyard, and he tucked his golden wings tightly behind him. The girl waiting for him there was lovely with long, flowing blond hair, icy blue eyes, tall frame, and shapely but lean body. She could bring him what no other could. She was the shield maker. She could give him a place to rest, a zone where his blood would not call to every thirsty Akhkharu and Nephilim in the world.

Belial, Ini-herit's father, was attractive. That was his power. Belial had been a deceptively beautiful Gregori whose name meant "without worth." While Ki's other sons and lovers had abilities that were useful, Belial was a temptation to every man, woman, human, Gregori, Shinar, Nephilim, and Akhkharu alive. Everyone wanted to possess him, consume his life. Belial had learned to reverse the ability, repelling anyone, keeping them away.

Ini-herit had never learned that trick. He was constantly on the run. The shield maker could change that. She *would*, too, no matter what Ini-herit had to do or say to ensure her devotion to him.

CHRISTY WATCHED as the Nephilim landed just feet from her and the two toddlers. He was the most beautiful thing she'd ever seen. His skin had a glossy sheen to it and was a rich bronze color. His wings were also metallic seeming, but not just from the sun. They were especially alluring with their flecks of gold leaf that reflected the light. His broad shoulders created a most pleasing contrast to his narrow waist and hips. He was nude and Christy quickly looked away from *that* area, though it was as perfect as the rest of him.

He was totally hairless, body and head the same color. His face was regal, large black eyes topped a long thin nose and a generous mouth. He looked like the image of Egyptian pharaohs she'd seen in her history books before she'd dropped out of school. He was just missing the kohl around his eyes and an ankh-topped scepter. His only ornament was an odd-looking necklace made of a single, but large, red stone on a leather string.

Christy was glad she'd gotten a little sun over the last few months and she wasn't that same pasty, bruise-mottled girl Maeve and Aaron had saved a few years ago. She wasn't tan by any means, but she looked healthy. She wished she'd worn something better than her jean cutoffs and racerback tank top. At least the top's light blue color complimented her eyes, and she had her makeup on. She never went anywhere without her war paint. She stood on her toes to make her legs look as shapely as possible and puffed out her chest.

"Quickly make your shield around us." His voice was as attractive as his body. Like all the Nephilim who had flocked to live near the One, his voice was an enigma, completely bizarre and yet somehow pleasant, like music made from street noise. It was hard to tell if there were two or three voices coming from his mouth, but it was definitely more than one.

As soon as he spoke, all thoughts were flung from her mind. She couldn't worry about what he wanted or what she looked like. She couldn't think of anything other than him, touching him, tasting him, possessing him. Goddess, how she wanted him.

The golden god began to look around himself. Sam was standing now and staring intently at the newcomer. Other Nephilim were gathering too. He turned to her, desperation in his eyes. His eyes! They weren't just black as she had originally thought. They were multicolored jewels just as the other Nephilim's but where theirs were white opals, his were black opals. The dark background made the colors much more vibrant. Christy thought it looked like the telescope photos of nebulae she'd seen in school. As soon as she thought it, the colors began to swirl, pulling her and everything into their very center. He shouted, "Your shield! Quickly, or I will be forced to flee."

He'd broken the spell and hit a nerve. She would do *anything* to keep him close to her. Flee? No, she couldn't let that happen. "I need a circle," she replied, her voice barely above a whisper.

He put his wings back out, their tips poking down. He dug them into the ground and spun around. Their tips made a circular rut in the manicured lawn. He held his hand out to her. Christy couldn't help but step forward and place her hand in his. He pulled her body against him, draping his arm softly around her, as if he were afraid of crushing her. "Shield us, please. I must be alone with you."

His words made her quiver. She wanted that too. She didn't need to say the words aloud anymore, but she thought them. *Kiyahwe will not allow you to hurt her children.* With a flick of her wrist, the mini personal shield was up. His shoulders dropped a fraction of an inch, and his sigh brushed the top of her head. He lifted her feet off the ground with an arm around her waist and rested his head on her shoulder. He seemed to be smelling her skin. When he spoke, his breath tickled her ear. "I will never let you go. I have searched the world for your kind." He choked on his words a little, and Christy thought she might have sensed guilt in the statement.

It was by far the most romantic thing she had ever heard, much less that anyone had ever said to her in all her eighteen, almost nineteen years. She licked the bead of sweat running down his neck because she couldn't help herself and was surprised when it tasted sweet like honey. She nipped her way up to his earlobe.

Sam cleared his throat. Christy had forgotten anyone else was around. "I will take the little ones in for their bath. You need time to celebrate. The finding of one's Sinnis is a special occurrence indeed."

She didn't answer. She knew Sam would take good care of Genevieve and Juliet. Whatever his reasons for hesitations with the latter, Sam would never hurt a child. She wasn't worried and gave it no thought. Her attention was on her Nephilim. She rubbed against him like a cat in heat. She'd never felt desire anywhere near this level, except when she'd learned to make her shield.

Christy hadn't been born into the Daughters. She had not grown up knowing that she was special, that she could work magic using the white energy generated from matched couples around the world. She had been an ordinary girl. Her mother had raised her as best she could, all on her own. Her father had left when she was just a baby. She didn't know much about him except his name. He was just the first in a long line of men who had not wanted her, had not thought her special enough to stick around.

She had searched her whole life for someone, anyone, who wanted her more than anyone else. She had a string of boyfriends a mile long, all of which were promising at first, and then, when the newness dwindled, so had their affections. She did more and more to please them and that was how she'd found herself in the position that Aaron and Maeve had saved her from, bent over a picnic table in the backyard of someone she didn't know, ready to be gangbanged by Hunter and his idiot friends. She had only been seventeen.

Hunter had been Christy's last boyfriend. His abuse had escalated so quickly that she hadn't even seen it for what it was until Nathalia had told her he was in jail. He had beaten her, convinced her she deserved it, even wanted it. That was when she had amped up the level of makeup she wore. Her bruised and battered face had needed it. Hunter had recently added public humiliation to the mix when she went to that party with him and his boys. There had been twelve of them and when they went out into the backyard for a smoke, she'd known what was going to happen.

She still had nightmares about that night: the feel of so many hands on her body, the rough wood on her face. The worst part was that she hadn't even fought them. Thank goddess that Aaron and Maeve had shown up. Aaron had ripped a piece of weathered board off the nearby fence and whacked Hunter right across the cheek. Maeve somehow subdued the rest of them with tasers and pepper spray.

After that Christy had come to live with the Daughters, first in their battered women's shelter and then onto the main compound but not into their ranks. There were no other shield makers. There was no one to mentor her. Without a mentor she couldn't be initiated. It barely mattered. She knew their most important secrets, same as if she were amongst their highest rank.

Here on the compound, she had only two responsibilities in addition to the shielding. The first was her bi-monthly counseling sessions for the trauma she'd lived through. The second was watching the toddlers while their mothers did their chores. Sometimes there were just the two and other times as many as six. No one thought she had any magical ability until the day their compound was attacked.

She had been standing in almost the same place that day that she and the golden Nephilim stood now. She had gathered the young children to play in the shade of the grove during the heat of the day. They had their shoes off, feeling the thick, soft, cool grass. The little ones had been fascinated by the ring of tiny mushrooms in the clearing. Christy had been having trouble keeping them all from tasting them. Kids put everything in their mouths, but she didn't know anything about mushrooms and was worried they might be poisonous. So she distracted them with a story about fairy rings that her grandma used to tell her as a kid.

The military-like men had moved past her then. Christy had known they were out of place, unwelcome here amongst the peaceful Daughters. She was not really worried because no soldier would hurt a girl with a bunch of babies. She had been wrong because as they passed there had been one man who'd pointed a gun at her. She'd gotten mad, madder than she'd ever been. She'd thought, how dare he threaten those precious innocent babies! They didn't even know enough to be scared, for goddess sakes.

It was like she had a sudden flash of a memory she hadn't known was there. She had been thinking of her grandmother. She'd remembered Gramma saying this, so she'd said the same words she used every time since then to call up her shield. She'd used the power lines that only she could see and in doing so had discovered the Daughters' secret. She'd shielded them all, first the babies and then everyone who lived within the compound's walls, using her unique ability. Now, this Nephilim said that she was more than special. He had searched the whole world for thousands of years for her kind and she was the only one he'd found.

"I want you," she found herself saying.

Her Nephilim sighed again, his shoulders lowering a little more. "I know. I must rest and I have not fed for many months." His lips made a burning hot trail along her neck and made her shiver with a need she could not name.

He took off with one great flap of his wings, their shield bursting as soon as Christy touched its edge. A few seconds later they landed on the top of the great three-story library. The Daughters had converted an old mission to suit their coven's needs and the library was the old turret and bell tower. Its roof was flat and its walls circular so she had her circle. Christy put up a new shield as soon as her feet touched the stones. The entire rooftop was theirs alone.

The Nephilim moved away from her so quickly that she almost lost her balance in the void he'd left. She stumbled but caught herself. Christy watched his back as he stretched to his full wingspan before tucking the gilded airfoils behind him again. They pulled at her and she couldn't resist them. She laid her ear on one shoulder blade and looked at the place on the other one from which the wing grew. "The other Guardians hide their wings," she whispered as she fingered their soft bat-like flesh. They weren't made of feathers like the angels of the Bible.

A shudder rippled down from her touch and her Nephilim sighed again. "One cannot be a Guardian with nothing to protect. I'm a Nephilim, and a useless one at that. My brother could shield, but he is lost to us now. He is Akhkharu." He spun, wrapping his wings around them both so that they stood in a booth made of his body. The light filtering through his wings made her skin look as golden bronze as his. "You smell like him, but so very different. The human in you calls out more strongly than any woman I've met. There is no mistaking your lineage. You are a woman from our mother's line."

He was saying she was a Sinnis, Christy was sure. Nathalia and Maeve had warned her that the Nephilim were all searching for certain magical women from specific family trees. Those women would drink the blood of their Nephilim and be forever changed. Her eyes went to the necklace that hung in the hollow of his throat. It was his birthmark, a gift from his human mother and Gregori father. It was to be a gift to his Sinnis. Sinking into her flesh, it would mark her as his and give her untold power. Christy wanted it.

She nuzzled her cheek against his chest and took his small, flat nipple into her mouth. He moaned a little but he didn't stop her. She laid kisses along a path to the other side as her hands worked their way toward the ruby stone on the leather thong. She closed her palm around the stone and it glowed and pulsed. Christy opened her mouth and prepared to bite down on his pectoral. She had to taste his blood for the conversion to happen. Her arms and mouth were suddenly empty, and she almost fell again in the void he'd left.

She was annoyed until he grabbed her from behind. "You can't," was all he said, but his breath on her skin was electrifying. Her clothes were almost painful now and she pulled at them. He sensed her discomfort and eased the offending garments from her. She felt weak and then the world was fuzzy. The next few hours were a blur to her but she knew several things. She was as nude as her Nephilim. He was hungry for her, insatiable. And as many times as he brought her to climax with his mouth, something was incomplete, unfulfilled.

When the sun set, her Nephilim was anxious, and she asked him why. He wrapped his sparkling wings around them both where they rested on the roof and told her, "It has been many centuries since I have felt safe to sleep in the cool of the night." He kissed Christy on the top of her head.

She snuggled closer to him, but his scent was intoxicating, and she found herself clawing at his chest and face. He effortlessly held her at a distance. She wanted him, sexually and in another indistinguishable way. Then she had the craziest thought: he was being selfish. But that idea was insane. He had gone down on her for hours and asked nothing in return. That was the opposite of a selfish lover, wasn't it? She could not shake the feeling that all of that had been for himself, without any real concern for her needs at all. She knew he had what she wanted but wouldn't give it to her. She laughed out loud at how insane she sounded and was glad his ability was not mind reading.

"What is so funny, shield maker?" His voice sounded groggy, and it made Christy yawn.

She decided on the lie since it was a thing she also found queer. "After all…that, we don't even know each other. I'm—"

"My salvation," he interrupted her. He laid infuriatingly soft kisses on her face.

"Yeah, I know all about the Sinnis business. I was talking about names. I'm Christy Adams." She waited, but when no answer came immediately, she flat out asked him, "What should I call you?"

The pause was long enough to make Christy uneasy. Was he actually considering not giving her his name? After she'd let him bury his face in her snatch, was he going to give her a fake name? She tried to sit up. She wanted to walk away from him, wanted to argue with him, but she couldn't. He was like a magnet. She knew she wanted him more than she wanted anything else. She would take any abuse he doled out as long as he let her stay beside him. That was yet another subject for her bi-monthly session with Nathalia.

"Belial Maru, the elder. You may call me Belial." When she looked up at him questioningly, he added, "It's a family name. Your family."

TWO

The being who had been William Cunningham before being torn in half tested his new legs. Near weightless, they made him fast and strong and whole again. The Shinar, though they insisted he not use that name in their presence, had miraculous powers. They were God. Maybe they weren't exactly the Trinity of the Bible, but they were the real deal. The Bible was filtered through the limited minds of humans, after all. There were bound to be some inaccuracies.

Those Who See and Observe, who refused to take names, Shinar or otherwise, had cared for Will after saving him from the earth witch. So powerful was Tara Kay that Will, in his human life, had thought he loved her. He knew better now. She was a demon. Or if not by that name, she was at least the enemy of God, so what did that make her?

Will was now the chosen vessel for Those Who See and Observe. They had another before him, the woman named Nathalia, but she had chosen to follow a Nephilim named Eiran and the Shinar had to abandon hope that she would fulfill her destiny. That destiny now belonged to Will. He could open the veil to let them through. He could wield the dagger for them. Once he stained it with the blood of an unclaimed Sinnis, it would be a weapon to match him: unstoppable.

He looked around what seemed to be a nursery. A nursery with walls made of rough cut stones, no less. The arches and heavy wooden doors with rounded tops screamed catholic mission. He was here to kill Ishtar, the One the humans would worship and the Shinar feared so much. Luckily, she was housed where the veil was thin enough that a human could be pushed through. Those Who See and Observe could not come through here. The bloodshed had not been the right kind or in high enough levels, though the blood of the First had almost done it. In addition to that, the shield maker was here. She could easily repair the veil and once that was done, this portal would be dead. The Shinar used it sparingly. Will knew he was the second man, and would be the last, to be pushed through it.

They had told him that time passed differently in their realm. He didn't know how long it had been on earth while he was with the Shinar. He didn't know where he was, but the warm air coming through the window told him it was summer. He approached the bed. They hadn't told him Ishtar would be so small. He should just stab through the small, covered mound, but he needed to see. He pulled down the sheet.

It was just a toddler. Two years old, maybe three. The letters on the wall above her bed said her name was Genevieve. Will lifted the dagger, ready to murder an innocent. And then something happened. He couldn't kill her. He wanted to leave, to run, to never look back. The dagger did not want that. It had a way of getting what it wanted. His arm lashed out, slicing through the tiny palm resting on the mattress over her dark hair.

She screamed.

Will stared at her, at the red that coated the dagger's edge and the red that soaked her blankets. The bedding was an odd texture. The plain unbleached cotton threads, handwoven into a simple fabric seemed out of place in the modern world. Then again, everything in this nursery seemed out of place between the ancient stone walls. Perhaps the Shinar had sent him back in time to destroy Ishtar. He did not think bending of time, nor any other action, was beyond the realm of possibility, not when the Shinar were involved.

He felt the pull and disappeared back into the tear in the veil he had come through. He was back with Those Who See and Observe, all thoughts of Ishtar gone. He hadn't killed her, but the dagger was coated. It was now DakuAhu, the "kill-brother." The Shinar would be happy enough that it could be used to kill the half-breeds.

HARITH SAMSIEL Maru watched as the Shinar's new warrior stepped back through the tear in the veil between this world and theirs. Sam, as he let the Daughters call him, held the One, the sleeping Genevieve, in his arms and used his camouflage to mask them both from detection. He had been nearly invisible to the man who was now gone with what he thought was a DakuAhu.

The child who had been injured screamed, but he made no move to comfort her. She was not his priority. Once Genevieve was awakened by the noise, he only had care for her well-being. Sam held the One close and soothed her with voice and touch. She had never been affected by the odd tingle in his touch. She was made to absorb that energy that he could so easily share. She was of his mother's bloodline. Genevieve was his Sinnis Ina Ummum Zumru, his woman from mother's body.

Aaron, Genevieve's father, burst into the room in nothing but his boxers. He ran to the bed and scooped up the crying other girl. "What happened? She's covered in blood, Sam!" He was still trying to ascertain where all that blood was coming from when two more people came barreling in.

Jolie, the injured toddler's mother, blanched at the sight of her child in such a condition. Her skin paled, making her many tattoos seem all the more dark by comparison. She took the child from Aaron's arms, who continued to search for the source of all that blood. JD, the father, joined him in his quest. When they were certain that it was only from the wound in her hand and nothing more serious, and they had fashioned a bandage from the already ruined bedclothes, they three in unison turned to Sam, who was sitting quietly rocking Genevieve.

"What happened?" Jolie demanded.

Sam shrugged. "I kept him from killing her."

"You kept who from killing her?"

"I protected the One."

"And as always with you, that is all that matters. The rest of us be damned, as long as your future mate is safe?"

"Yes." Sam looked back to Genevieve, visibly dismissing them all.

JD, ever reasonable, stepped between his wife and the giant. "Come on, angelface. We need to get Juliet to the healer."

"I am not leaving until he tells me what happened. Why is *my* baby bloody but *Maeve's* is perfectly fine?"

"I protect what is mine," Sam sang, never looking up at her.

"There's nobody here but you." She looked around the room sarcastically. "No murderous men that I can see."

"He was not a man. A half man, half Shinar."

Jolie eyed him suspiciously. "YOU are a half man, half Shinar. Did you hurt her, *half-breed*?"

The three parents saw the fire flare in Sam's eye at the insult and only Jolie was unafraid. She was a mother whose baby had been hurt. At that moment she wasn't afraid of anything. She wanted someone to pay for her Juliet's tears.

"You know what your child will become. You say nothing because you are blinded by a mother's love. It would be better for all of us if she had died in your womb. I should have let the half man kill her."

"How dare you come into our home and say such things!"

"It is my home too."

"No, it isn't. Daughters *allow* you to stay nearby because you said we were in danger. You said we needed Nephilim protection. I am starting to think we need protection *from* you. We should banish you all."

Sam bared his teeth, sharp and dangerous now. "Try to force me from the One and I will stop at nothing to get back to her. No shield maker could keep me away." A rumbling, not unlike that of a lion, came from his chest and he made no effort to stop it.

Aaron stepped in to defuse the situation. The giant was holding his daughter, after all. "I won't let that happen, Sam. I know how you feel about Genevieve. Maybe you could tell us exactly what happened. Sometimes knowing the facts is the best way to settle nerves."

"I must speak with the First. She alone will know what to do." Sam handed Genevieve to Aaron. "Do not stay in this room. It is not safe." He herded them into the outer room and took a plant from the window and put it next to the now closed nursery door. He pointed and said, "If that wilts, even in the slightest amount, take her into the Holy Capacitors room," then disappeared in that way only Nephilim could. He tabalu'd, dissolving himself down to the cellular level and moved through the earth only to reappear wherever he needed to.

"I hate when he does that." Aaron handed Genevieve to JD to hold while he put some clothes on. "Let's all go see Camilla. She can heal just about anything and with that magic blood of Nanae, there won't even be a scar."

"No. Hell, no, Aaron. We're taking her to the hospital for stitches. If she has to grow up with Nephilim all around her, maybe she needs a physical reminder of how dangerous they truly are. When we get back, I am going to have a serious talk with Christy." Where was that girl when this happened? She was supposed to be watching Juliet and Genevieve, not leaving them with an unstable demigod.

"WHAT IS it? Did something happen to Genevieve?" Maeve was panicked. Sam was Genevieve's Guardian and he never left her side. Seeing him appear so far from the compound meant that something serious must have happened. Sam stared at her for a minute before she remembered. "Oh, yes, I'm Lilitu now." She waived it away. "Never mind that. We'll talk about it later. Where's Genevieve?"

Sam remembered himself and knelt, his wings spread out behind him, trailing in the dirt. "Mother, the One is quite safe and unharmed. She is with Father. But I must speak to the First."

I am here, Harith Samsiel Maru. Nathalia spoke in her unique way. Her vocal cords were destroyed and through her magic and the magic of Eiran's blood, she had the ability to put her thoughts, her words and feelings, into the minds of others.

Maeve rubbed at her chest, the phantom wounds throbbing. "Sam, when you're done, can you fly me home?" She needed to get to the Daughters' compound in Austin. She had almost died the previous night when a murderous man from the Paion had stabbed her repeatedly. By consuming Nathalia and Tara's Sinnis blood, she was made into a Lilitu, a kind of succubus that was immortal, but needed to consume sexual energy for nourishment. She needed to get to Aaron. She hoped that being a Levitus would enable him to feed her. Back home, Izzy, the only male Lilitu known and mate of Camilla and Nanae, could help her adjust to her new life and teach her to use her newfound abilities.

"Certainly, Holy Mother. I live to serve you and your daughter." Sam was eager to get back to his Sinnis as she was yet unclaimed and vulnerable but flying would only take a little longer than tabalu. They weren't physically that far from home. He stood and, together with Nathalia, watched Maeve walk away. "The Shinar have a new dagger. It can slice through the veil, but it is not DakuAhu." He spoke softly, only Nathalia could hear.

Nathalia turned to him. She knew they had the dagger. She had watched as the Shinar tore Will Cunningham in half in a tug of war with Kiyahwe to get it only last night. *Yes,* she said, *but how do you know about it?*

"Only moments ago, a man, human from the waist up and pure Shinar energy below, stepped through the veil between our world and theirs. He was wielding the dagger."

So the Shinar had found a replacement warrior, she thought. Nathalia, Ereshkigal, in a previous life, was their chosen champion, but she had seen their plan and rejected them. Now they had chosen again and were attempting to recreate the DakuAhu. The "kill-brother" was a weapon made of Shinar bone and bathed in the blood of human, Akhkharu, and unclaimed Sinnis, and it was capable of what none other, save Nathalia herself, could do. It could kill the immortal Nephilim. It collected the prana, the life, from their nonhuman half, life that was stolen from the Shinar when Yahwe had separated Herself from them and created a race of lovers, called the Gregori, for Herself. They, in turn, had abandoned Her for their human wives and birthed the half-breed Nephilim.

"He was there to kill the One, but, as his mind is pure human, I was able to hide Genevieve's presence in my own camouflage."

Then they will try to get to her again. There was no stopping the Shinar in their attempt to make the DakuAhu nor ending their desire to kill the One. Genevieve was going to be humanity's savior. How, they weren't quite sure.

"No. They believe they have succeeded. I let him take the blood of another, thinking it was the One."

You let him KILL another baby? There was only one child the same age as Genevieve on the compound where they all lived. *Juliet? You let him kill Jolie's baby girl?*

Sam shook his head. "A flesh wound only. I filled him with the desire to leave her alive, but he returned to the Shinar thinking he had bathed the dagger in unclaimed Sinnis blood, the blood of the One, and that he had made a new DakuAhu."

You bought us time. How much, I don't know. Time passed differently in the plane where the Shinar lived. Nathalia had herself been there with them. She'd spent years, an entire lifetime, away only to return and find mere hours had passed on earth. *We must get back. Eiran will tabalu us. You must fly Maeve home.*

She turned to go, but Sam's hand on her arm stopped her. "There is more."

Sam had never touched Nathalia before, and she was stunned to find it pleasing. It filled her with a similar tingle to Eiran's. The only other Nephilim to touch her had been Eitan, Eiran's brother turned Akhkharu. He had died the final death; Nathalia had absorbed his prana. It had gathered in her birthmark, the stone from Eiran that had sunken below her flesh, just as if she were a living, breathing DakuAhu.

Eiran's weight crashed into Sam. Nathalia rolled her eyes, but allowed them to fight for a moment before using her knowledge and abilities to bind them. The two Nephilim froze, their feet, to the ankles, encased in the mother earth. She left them there. Males, no matter what the species, were so predictable. Possessive to the core, Eiran had reacted with murder in his heart that any other had laid a hand on his Sinnis. Nathalia did love Eiran. There was no denying it, but some of his attitudes were from the dark ages. She chuckled when she thought of how much older than the Middle Ages he was at over 7,000 years old.

She gestured that Sam should speak.

"Another Sinnis has been found. Christy, the shield maker."

Who has claimed her?

"He arrived only today, and I did not know him. He glows like none other I have ever seen, almost as if he secretes gold dust. It is difficult to describe him, as I am sure he was using camouflage, but he was very attractive. I, myself, felt his pull before the shield maker used her magic to cut him off from the rest of us."

Nathalia knew of the Nephilim that Sam had seen. It could only be Ini-herit Belial Maru. It was odd that she had no history with the Nephilim, not even from her life as Ereshkigal. She knew the true names and power of all Nephilim and this one was no different, but she did wonder why Ereshkigal had no run-ins with him. Nathalia had met him once before and felt the attraction herself. The desire to sink her teeth into his golden flesh and swallow down his sweet blood in great gulps was undeniable. His aroma was intoxicating and enticing enough to tempt any Nephilim to break their first and most sacred law. Never were they to drink the blood of another Nephilim nor taste their flesh because to do so would make them Akhkharu. Being in the presence of Ini-herit Belial Maru had been so seductive that Nathalia, the very maker of that law, had considered breaking it.

Eiran spoke inside her mind, *Mine is the only Nephilim blood you will ever taste, and I find it hurts me to hear your desire for this other.* Nathalia was of Eiran's mother's family line. It wasn't incest when talking about 360 generations, but it meant that they shared the same abilities. They were both telepathic.

I am sorry Eiran. I did not mean to hurt you. My desire for Iniherit is artificial, something to do with his ability. Do not take it to heart. She turned to Sam and put the conversation back on course. *How do you know Christy is the golden one's Sinnis?*

"I saw them together. There was an instant spark. I can only hope that when Genevieve is of age that she will look at me in the manner Christy looked at her Nephilim."

CHRISTY WOKE up sweating. She shivered despite the warm night air. There was only one thing that caused the vibrating feeling she had awoken to. She reached for the alarm button she wore around her neck at night. But it wasn't there; she wasn't in her room. She and Belial had fallen asleep on the roof, so she hadn't gone through her normal bedtime routine.

She sat up and took a few deep breaths. The vibrations were the result of someone coming in contact with her shield, but unlike previous times, this touch wasn't malicious. It was more like someone was stroking the shield, admiring her work. The touch was like a caress and it made her tingle. Some parts of her body felt light as air while her womb felt heavy but empty at the same time. Her thoughts went to the Akhkharu.

She looked, but the location of the shield touch was too far away. It was the same place that she had met the monster who could cloak himself. The whole area was hidden in shadow but she thought she saw a flash of red, two circles side by side. They were gone as quickly as they had appeared, like roadside reflectors under the headlights of a passing car. It…no, he was watching her. She stood and walked to the wall's edge, closest to the place she'd seen the red eyes.

The caress changed then. The tempo quickened and her breathing went ragged. She rubbed roughly at her own breasts before trailing her right hand down over her stomach and then slipped a finger inside. She didn't bother with her clit; it was like whatever was caressing her shield was rubbing that nodule for her. She wanted to be filled.

She pumped two fingers and then three in and out of her pussy, but even that wasn't enough. Pressure was building. Her orgasm was not far off. Her other hand still rubbed at her breasts, pulling at her nipples. She moved it up over her neck and then into the hair on the back of her head. She fisted a great handful and then tugged it back. That little slice of violence, that echo of passion, was enough to finish her off.

IMENDAND BELIAL Maru stood and watched from the shadows as the girl on the rooftop, Christy, brought herself to climax. He enjoyed the show she put on. His eyes glowed red with hunger for her. He would find a way to get to her. He would sink his teeth into her soft flesh and feast on her blood.

His vrykolak pack whimpered from the bushes and Fox, his chosen alpha, growled at them for silence. Imendand knew they needed to hunt, to run and chase, to kill. They were hungry for the prana-rich flesh of the living, but they would have to wait. Imendand had found her and wanted to bring her pleasure that she would remember and long for, pleasure that would bring her running into his cruel, waiting arms. It was pleasure he knew she could not gain from his brother's loving ones.

AS THE fireworks subsided, Christy noticed her leg was shaking. She felt weak, but the caress was still going. She made a frustrated sound in the back of her throat when it cut off suddenly. Belial stood beside her and she dropped her hands quickly, ashamed he'd caught her masturbating. "What's wrong?" he asked. "I heard you cry out."

"Nothing. I thought someone was trying to breach the shield, but it was nothing."

He looked at her, the disbelief clear in his multi-colored opal eyes. "What does it feel like when someone tries to come through uninvited?"

Christy thought about how aroused she had been only seconds ago and decided not to tell him about that. "When someone with malice in their heart touches it, there's pain."

"So evil people hurt. And when they are good?"

Christy didn't bother telling him that there are no purely evil or completely good people. The world wasn't black and white, but shades of gray. "Hasn't happened. Nathalia tells me about anyone she wants able to come and go and I don't feel it at all. No one has ever had to try to come through in secret that didn't have bad intentions. If they did, they got through and I never knew it." Christy shrugged. She didn't want to talk about this anymore. She was done with foreplay. She wanted the main event. She hadn't had any sexual contact with anyone since coming to stay with the Daughters except her own hand and the dildo she'd named "Edward" after that tool in the book all the girls her age fawned over. The strange vibrations of her shield had stirred something in her that was not yet satisfied.

Belial took her hand and pulled her back to their makeshift bed, a pile of towels left up there for sunbathers. Instead of settling down beside him as he expected, she straddled his thighs and took matters into her own hand, so to speak. Before she had two strokes in, long before he was hard enough to use the way she wanted, Belial had her on her back, arms pinned at her sides. "What are you doing?"

"I thought it was pretty obvious. Don't you want to…?" She left the question hanging unfinished because she couldn't bring herself to say it.

"No. I mean yes," he altered quickly when her face fell. "I do, but it wouldn't be right. You are not my…old enough."

"I'm an adult," she insisted. "And it's not like I'm a virgin. You don't have to be so gentle with me. I won't break."

"You may have been with men, but they were human, not Nephilim, so you are a virgin of sorts. I will, very much so, have to be gentle with you. You are quite breakable. You are much too valuable to risk." Christy didn't look like she was buying his excuse. He tried another. "I would have our first time be special."

"It will be special," she begged, hating how whiny she sounded. It almost sounded childish.

Belial sounded mad when he cut off her pleading. "Not tonight. Go to sleep, Christy. I'll not hear another word about it." He wrapped her in the luxurious softness of his wing, effectively cutting her off from the rest of his body, and then turned his back to her.

He made an irritated noise when she ran her tongue across the top edge of that wing. She made suggestive movements with her body and traced enticing designs on the inside of his wing with her hands. She wouldn't talk about it, but that didn't mean she would stop trying to win him over to her side of things. She didn't say, but being bound like this was making her more horny, not less.

THREE

Nathalia had called Christy into Maeve's office. It wasn't really an office, but a converted side chapel that they had used as a conference room before. It had more room, was still conveniently located, and served very well. They needed an office with more space because, though Maeve was Abbess, she and Nathalia shared the tasks of that position. Maeve kept normal business hours here and she kept her toddler with her. With Genevieve came her Guardian, Harith Samsiel Maru. Aaron, Genevieve's dad and Maeve's mate, was also there today. Nathalia was in attendance and with her came her Nephilim, Eiran Kafziel Maru. Guardians called Nathalia the First and Genevieve the One. They were both something special to the Nephilim but the what and how weren't really clear. They were all involved with decisions that affected Daughters and Nephilim and so the much larger office was already crowded even before people came in to have an audience with them. Today Jolie was with them and she looked angry.

Belial hadn't wanted to answer the summons, but Christy had promised to shield him, knowing that she couldn't ignore Nathalia. Belial was used to living in the wild, sleeping in the safety of sunlight on mountaintops and flying in the dark, dangerous night. He was still nude and had his wings visible. He followed her closely and she was glad she couldn't get mesmerized by his dazzling good looks. He pulled a chair into the center of the room and sat. He pulled Christy into his lap and made a large circle around them with his massive wingspan, which he relaxed once the shield was in place.

Christy was nervous. She had never been called into what the younger girls had named the throne room. It did look that way, with the raised dais at the front holding three ornately carved chairs. It was where priests and cardinals held council when this place was a working mission. It was probably designed to instill a sense of guilt and anxiety.

Maeve sat in one of the velvet upholstered chairs with Aaron standing close by her. She seemed distracted by his nearness. Nathalia sat in the one to her right with Jolie standing on the other side, at the edge of the raised platform. The third was empty, but Eiran and Sam sat on the floor behind it, with Genevieve playing sandwiched between them. The two Guardians kept her from coming to Christy when the toddler saw her favorite babysitter.

Christy spoke first. "Where's Juliet?"

"Oh, so now you care?" Jolie's voice dripped with venom.

Nathalia explained before Christy could comprehend what had Jolie so angry. *Juliet was hurt last night while you were with your Nephilim.*

"Oh, goddess. Is she okay?"

She will be. She needed stitches, but it was just a flesh wound.

"How? What happened?"

That is actually what we need to talk to you about. You are in a unique position to help, not only us but the whole world. You see, the earth and all its inhabitants are shielded by a veil. That veil has been...

"Wait," Jolie interrupted. "That's it? My baby had to spend the night in the emergency room because this girl shirked her one responsibility so she could get laid, and you aren't even going to fuss!"

Nathalia spoke to them all at once. She was capable of speaking to large groups, people at a distance, isolated telepathy, and even conversing with only a few select people in a crowd. *You don't understand the pull a Nephilim has on his Sinnis, especially at first. If seeing him for the first time was as overwhelming as it was for me, she couldn't think clearly. It will…*

"That's exactly what I am talking about. If we can't be trusted to act rationally with creatures around us, maybe they shouldn't be allowed here. Maeve, wake up! Look around; we're surrounded. The Daughters aren't following our own creed. You're the Abbess. Send them away and let's get back to doing the founders' work."

Maeve spoke then, scarcely able to pull her eyes from Aaron. "Jolie, you know I can't do that. The founders didn't have the whole story. We have a grander place in the scheme of things than they originally thought."

Christy had never seen Jolie so worked up. She was normally such a quiet woman. Her appearance was at such odds with her shy nature. Red crept up her neck and face, and even down her arms, obscuring the lines of her many tattoos and somehow lessening the shock of her pink hair.

Jolie stormed out, but Maeve stopped Nathalia when she stood to follow. "Let me talk to her. I can understand what she's feeling. I'd be furious if my daughter had been the one hurt because someone shirked their responsibility." She turned to Christy then. "That can never happen again."

"N…no, ma'am. It won't."

"I know, Christy. You are a good nanny. We all make mistakes, but sometimes when we do, we have to pay for them." She put her hands on the carved arms of her chair as if to push up but seemed to think of something. A panicked look crossed her face. Aaron stood, smiled at her, and held out his hand. Maeve visibly relaxed, took what was offered, and the two of them left. Maeve was new to her Lilitu nature and could easily hurt those around her. Aaron was her anchor and her sustenance.

I think it would be best if you had a break. We will give you two weeks' vacation from your normal duties. It will give you time to get to know your Nephilim and become accustomed to his influence. This is not a punishment. Think of it as a honeymoon of sorts, and be glad you have the Daughters' compound to enjoy it. That is luxury compared to the tomb I spent mine in.

Eiran spoke only to his Sinnis in her mind. *I don't recall you complaining about your treatment at my hands.*

Nathalia smiled at him. *No, no complaints about your hands, but it would have been nice to sleep in a real bed or go out.*

I took you out.

A day in the desert and a night fighting werewolves and zombies is not what I was talking about.

Thinking they were being dismissed, Belial stood, bringing Christy up with him.

Nathalia turned back to them and made apologies. *Before you go, can you please take a look at something for the Daughters?*

Christy nodded. Nathalia had asked, not ordered. Did she think Christy her equal now that Belial had claimed her? If only she knew how easily he dismissed and ignored Christy.

<hr />

SAM SAYS *the tear is in here, but I can't see it.* Nathalia and Christy and, of course, Belial, stood in the doorway of Genevieve's nursery. It had been Nathalia's private bedroom when she was Abbess. It was also where her human life had ended. She didn't enjoy being there, but Eiran absolutely refused to enter. It was where he had almost lost her again. He said the room reverberated with violence and he felt an echo of that moment when he'd thought she was dead and gone.

Christy concentrated, scanning the room. "I can." She pointed to the middle of the room. Only visible in her peripherals, it looked very similar to her shield. It didn't look like a tear, as she was expecting. If she thought about everything she saw as a curtain, that section was worn thin so that she could almost see through it. Shapes made of glittery light moved behind it, but she couldn't make them out. When she wasn't trying to see it, the shimmering disappeared.

That is exactly where Michael stepped through. Nathalia tried not to think of that horrifying moment when she'd seen her nightmare break through reality as easily as slicing through a movie screen. *I don't see anything now.*

"It's too light in here." Christy reached for the light switch, but Belial stopped her.

He stepped past the two women into the room. He knew the Shinar couldn't touch him. His unique half-breed prana couldn't be collected by them, no matter how close he got. Christy was human and another matter entirely. The Shinar had been known to suck a human dry from the other side if one got too close to a thin spot. He closed the shutters, blocking out as much sunlight as possible before cutting the lights. He stood in front of Christy. He wasn't taking any chances with his shield maker.

Christy found it nearly impossible to concentrate when Belial was so close and in her line of sight. His skin was so perfect. Golden dust was shed with even the smallest of movements and she could feel it all around her, thickening the air. The importance of what she was supposed to be doing was lost in the lusty haze. Her mouth salivated. She longed to open wide and take a chunk out of Belial's flesh. Would his meat taste as honeyed as his sweat? His wing, so close to her face, looked delicate, lacy almost, and made her think of the crispy airy texture and fried sweet taste of funnel cakes.

There it is. I can just barely make it out. It reminds me of... Christy, are you listening? Nathalia stopped speaking when she noticed the glazed over look in Christy's eyes. She grabbed Christy's hand and pulled her out through Maeve's living quarters into the sanctuary.

The room was large, and statues of women lined the walls. Three Nephilim were milling about near the door. Their eyes locked onto Belial as he followed the women. Nathalia led Christy to the center of the room where three concentric circles had been worn smooth into the flagstone floor. How many women had danced in the sacred circles for how many ceremonies for how many years to wear a groove in the stone with their bare feet, she could not speculate.

"Thank you," Belial said, seeing her plan. "Christy, your shield."

"Kiyahwe will not allow you to hurt her children," she muttered. A flick of her wrist and it was up with Nathalia and the other

Nephilim on the outside. Christy continued to daydream about feasting on Belial.

Nathalia snapped her fingers. When the girl didn't react, Nathalia used her broadcasting ability to push the desire to pay attention into Christy's mind. Christy seemed torn, but in the end, Nathalia's power could not be denied. *Can you fix it?*

Christy shook her head, as much to clear it as to indicate no. She was a one trick pony. She could make a shield, a bubble of protection and only if she were inside. That wouldn't help in this circumstance.

There are other thin spots that have been made into doorways, access restricted by a type of spell, like a black blanket, laid over it. Nathalia wished she could take Christy to see it, but knew if Christy left the grounds, the Daughters' shield would fall, leaving Genevieve, while not completely defenseless, less protected. It would be much easier if she could just show Christy. The shield maker might be able to "see" how the spell was constructed where Nathalia could just sense its complexity.

"A gisig, it is called, when the spell protects a tear," Eiran said as he approached.

This gisig is both the doorway and the doorman. It's contrived and cast to let certain people through and keep other ones out. I was allowed to pass through but the Shinar can no longer use that place as a doorway. They are barred. That could work here, couldn't it?

"I don't know how."

Goddess damn it! I wish we could find a mentor for you.

"There are none to be found," Belial uttered. It sounded sad, maybe even contrite, which confused them all. Why would he feel remorseful for the lack of shield makers? "That lineage died out in ancient Egypt."

No. When Kiyahwe spoke to us She said that there are others who can fix the veil between this world and her homeland. Others—plural. She said she can't see them anymore and that shielding was their gift. That means Christy should be able to fix the veil because she can shield, and she isn't the only one!

Eiran pulled Nathalia away. She was getting agitated. Nathalia was a warrior, a leader, and she hated feeling helpless, being unable to solve a problem, or unable to protect the ones she felt responsible for. "We will have the librarian search the archives again." He tucked his Sinnis under his wing, wrapping her in its soothing effect, and headed out into the courtyard.

BILLY WAS in the courtyard as usual, kneeling in the dirt, tending some plant others would overlook. He served as the Daughter's groundskeeper, but he was much more than that. He shared in their secrets. Billy had been born there and could not be forced away even though he was a male, because of that fact. Now he was mated to a Daughter and had an even greater claim as part of the group.

Dusting his hands off on his dark brown Carhartt's jacket, he jumped up when he saw Christy and the Nephilim come out of the sanctuary. He eyed the giant golden Nephilim who made no attempt to hide what he really was and approached them more cautiously than was normal for him. Most of the Guardians were overprotective of their Sinnis, bordering on obsessively possessive. Even with his newfound strength as a vrykolak, Billy had no desire to start a fight he had no hope of winning. When the glowing god made no move to stop him, Billy hugged Christy.

He was rewarded with a rare sight, Christy's smile. As always, her makeup was perfectly applied. Billy knew it served to make her feel safe, in some odd way. It was the same with her normal smirk, as if showing her teeth broke her facade, her defensive wall. Seeing those teeth now in a genuine, if small, grin, told Billy something good was happening in her life and that she had a chance to be truly happy.

So the rumors were true, he derived. Christy was this Nephilim's Sinnis. "Congrats, sis." Though they weren't actually related, Billy felt a kinship to her after his parents, Libby and Leonard, had taken her in. They loved her like the daughter they never had. Billy was their only child and they made that a conscious decision.

Women here were expected to birth at least one girl child to ensure the survival of their type of magic, which was only passed down from mother to daughter. Libby had known that with the value Daughters put on female children, if she had another, Billy would have been treated as a second-class citizen. She had endured much animosity in her endeavors to keep that from happening.

When Christy came, she stepped right into the void they hadn't known existed in their family. She had been through a lot and was badly damaged both physically and mentally and they had so much love to give. Billy never made a pass at her because he could see that Christy needed something else from him. She needed men to find value in her without sex. He was more than willing to provide that and felt that his family had aided in her recovery.

"Thanks. This is Belial." Her reply was uncharacteristically brief. She was embarrassed.

"Nice to meet you. I'm Billy." Billy stuck his hand out, but Belial just stood there. When it was clear Belial was going to leave him hanging, Billy lowered his hand. He fought to keep his attention on Christy and not her Nephilim. The man was exuding a serious sexual magnetism that was hard to ignore. "Minali wanted me to invite you to our rooms for a coffee ceremony tomorrow night." Minali was from Ethiopia. "It's traditional for welcoming family."

The winged man snapped to attention then. He took a step closer to the conversation and Billy couldn't keep from leaning in. "You are mated to the Siren? Minali is mated to a vrykolak?"

Billy wanted to puff out his chest and defend his place with his witch, but he couldn't manage it. He didn't want to offend the attractive half-breed. "Yes. She wants both of you to come over after dinner, after sunset." Everyone living on the compound was familiar with the habits of the Nephilim. Sunlight was very important to their health and they could not be enticed inside until after the source had sunk below the horizon. "She's made baklava for dessert especially for the occasion and if you haven't had it before, you'll have to trust me that it is amazing and well worth suffering my company to get at."

"I have tasted her sweet offerings before. We will join you tomorrow evening." With that, he wrapped one arm around Christy's waist and took to the sky. Only a few flaps of his massive wings and they were out of sight.

Billy wondered if it was a mistake to have them over after all. Something about the Nephilim had him uneasy.

FOUR

Bill Sagers silently cursed his goats as he made his way up the hill. They weren't where they were supposed to be and they hadn't come to the barn for milking. Goat cheese was a hot commodity recently. It sat well with those folks whose stomachs didn't agree with cow's milk. It was also hip with Austin's trendy restaurants for their hoity-toity goat cheese tartlets and such. Those damned goats made him more money than all his fourth-generation farming. He needed their milk and cheese in order to sell his organic spinach and tomatoes to those same restaurants.

Bill was too old and fat to go chasing after that idiot herd, he decided after losing his breath less than halfway up the hill. He knew if he got to the top, he could find them. From up there he could see for miles and miles of cleared brush. It was all pasture, hilly as it was. The hill country was hell on his knees, but the goats seemed to like it.

The farmer-come-rancher rested at the top and looked around. After he caught his breath, he called his son. "Bud, the damn goats are missing. Get in ya' truck and drive 'long tha fence lines. Maybe there's a break. Devil take 'em if they got in tha Pearson's corn field again. He'll probly take me ta' court this time." Bill paused to look at something in the distance. What the hell was that? "Come pick me up after. I don't wanna walk all the way back. I need ta' check somethin' out on the east field."

He closed his phone and started down. There was a small rise in the ground between what he considered the east and west field. It looked like there were heat waves coming up off the ground behind that swell. If a fire had started there, he'd need to know. He hoped the goats were smart enough to get out of the way of a grass fire. Dumb animals probably got themselves burned up.

As Bill neared the hill, he could see that the grasses were browned. Then he got close enough to see that they weren't burned. It was like someone had cut up sod from the land. Everything living was gone and just the brown dirt showed underneath. He went around the hill, rather than over it, to save some energy.

There, on the other side of that hill, lay the multicolored collars with bells he made his goats wear. They were just lying on the dry dirt, not in a pile, but just dropped here and there as if the beasts had managed to take them off and throw them down. No livestock to be seen. In fact, as Bill looked around, the area seemed oddly devoid of life. There were no plants in a fifty-foot radius, and the silence was deafening. Not a bird or squirrel or even toad or cicada made a sound.

He heard the running of water, but there weren't any streams near here. Something was wet near his foot and when he bent down, he knew it wasn't water. Dark red splashed onto his boots. Blood was bubbling up from the earth. It wasn't random, either. The blood was cutting little rivers in the dirt, making large concentric circles and small designs. The designs looked like rag-head or Jew writing to him.

Then Bill Sagers felt it. Light shone on his back and he turned to see its source. There was a thin line of light, brighter than anything he'd ever seen before, on the hillside. He stood, locked in that place, while the light shone happiness down on him. I must be looking at heaven, he thought.

The thin line was stretched and an arm, made of light, reached out to him. It was nowhere near his body, but Bill could feel the pull. His feet weren't moving, but he knew he was leaving this place and going wherever that hand wanted.

The euphoria was replaced by pain. He realized a moment too late that the light wasn't shining down on him. It was being pulled from him. He was powering the arm's glow with his life. Even with this epiphany, he could not turn away, could not run.

Bill Sagers ceased to be, his life force collected by the Shinar. His clothes collapsed into a pile on top of his boots and the area settled, waiting for the next meal to come by.

∞

THE NEW bed Nathalia ordered for Christy and Belial was very comfortable and large enough to accommodate his refusal to hide his wings. Even so, Christy couldn't sleep. She sat on the edge of that giant bed and looked over her shoulder at the sleeping Nephilim. His back was to her and she watched his side move up and down. She waited until his breathing slowed down before she stood.

She picked up the tee shirt and shorts that she'd worn earlier from the floor and put them on. The night was chilly, and she probably should try for something warmer, but she needed to get out before Belial woke. He had not allowed her out of his sight since arriving and she needed some air and some distance. She needed to clear her head. She didn't bother with socks. Slipping her tennis shoes on, she broke her shield and was out the door.

Silently she walked through the hall, down the stairs, and out into the courtyard. The grass was wet, shining in the moonlight, and Christy was glad she hadn't forgone the shoes. She made a beeline to the place she had felt the disturbance on her shield the previous night, the place where she'd seen the glowing red eyes. The beast had been there, watching her, caressing her shield and she wanted to be near that again. She wanted to hear the Akhkharu say that she was his again.

He was there, waiting, just as she knew he would be. He held out his hand, more of a paw with talons for fingernails, and gestured. "Come."

Christy realized she was drifting closer to him without having decided to. She took a step back and shook her head. "I can't. The shield breaks when I touch it. I have to have a circle and I have to stay inside that circle." She didn't tell him she could adjust the circle to allow different people to pass through. She had a feeling he could convince her to let him through and she knew that was a bad idea. She had already let something bad happen to Juliet. She might be banished by the Daughters if she let an Akhkharu on the grounds, especially if Genevieve was hurt.

"Those are limitations you put on yourself. Describe your process. What do you feel and see when you build it?"

Christy told him about the power lines flowing from all over. She hadn't known when she first used them, but now she did. These were made up of the sexual energy made by couples put together by the matchmakers like Maeve. This power was collected by the Capacitors, women who had given up this life in order to store power so that other Daughters could work their magic using it. They were a kind of living battery. She did not tell the Akhkharu about that. The Daughters kept their Capacitors very secret. They were vulnerable.

She told him what the lines were made of and he nodded as if it made perfect sense. She told him what she had to say and do to get the shield up. She told him about how it popped every time she touched its surface. He told her she needed to visualize the shield in her mind. It wasn't solid. It was made of threads that could be parted to allow her an opening.

Christy did not get a chance to test his technique. Nathalia's voice in her head sounded desperate. She was needed back in her room. Belial was causing a disturbance.

⁂

THE SCENE she found was very different from the peaceful one when she'd left Belial sleeping. Her Nephilim stood on the bed with his back against the wall. The Guardians standing in the hall and open doorway were leaning toward him, inching forward with every breath. Nathalia and Eiran were there just inside the door, short swords where their hands should have been, defending Belial's position.

Christy! Get in here and get that shield up. We can't hold them off much longer. Nathalia looked at Christy as the words sounded in her head.

Christy could see how dire this situation had become. She overcame her fear of all those sword arms and pushed through to get to Belial. She put her miniature room-sized shield up as soon as she was over the line etched in the stone of the floor. Only Nathalia and Eiran remained inside the circle. Slowly the Guardians, shielded from Belial's intoxicating allure, backed away. Some of them even shook their heads trying to clear their thoughts, their senses coming back to them as his influence diminished. A few even murmured apologies.

Nathalia and Eiran turned to them then, their sword hands reshaping into fingers, absorbing the metal back into their bodies. *Where were you?* Nathalia spoke to Christy but looked at Belial. The Sinnis known as the First actually licked her lips when her gaze dropped from Belial's face to his neck.

Belial held up his own sword hand and pointed it at the two of them who were drifting forward. "Maybe you should step back a foot or two," Christy suggested.

Once they were on the other side of the circle, Nathalia spoke again. *Even with Eiran's hunger beast sedated by my Sinnis blood, it was difficult not to attack you, Belial. The pull to consume you is all encompassing.*

"You must forgive the others. They are not as lucky as you and I to have found our Sinnis already. Their hunger, combined with your call, must be near impossible to resist." Christy wasn't sure she'd ever heard Eiran speak. His voice was like Sam's, a bizarre mix of the ugly combined into beauty.

Apologies made, Nathalia asked again, *Where were you, Christy?*

"I...I just went for a walk along the wall." She decided not to tell Nathalia about the Akhkharu. She told herself it was because she didn't want to worry Nathalia, but deep down she knew that it was because she didn't want Nathalia to stop her from going to him. Or worse, killing him so that Christy would never see him again.

This isn't like you, Christy. First that mess with Juliet and Genevieve and now this. I excused your behavior before because I can remember what it was like to be instantly smitten with your Nephilim but this... You have to think of the repercussions of your actions before you run off. You could have gotten your Nephilim injured. Those others could have been turned Akhkharu and then every one of the people who live here and count on us for protection would have been in danger.

"I didn't think anyone would know I slipped out. Honestly, I didn't think it would matter. I'm sorry. Really Nathalia, I am so sorry." Christy upturned her face to Belial, who was standing next to her. "I'm sorry, Belial. I didn't mean for you to get hurt."

He kissed the tip of her nose. The move infuriated Christy. She wanted something from Belial, some type of anger or passion. She wanted to be reprimanded by him, disciplined.

Being sorry is well and good, but it isn't going to cut it for long. Being a Sinnis is not all fairy tale romance. It is our destiny to be something, do something, bigger.

"I am weary." Belial spoke for the first time since Christy had come back to her room and found him under attack. His voice amplified the attraction to him. Maybe that was why he had kept silent for so long.

Nathalia shut the door quietly when Christy wrapped her arms around Belial's neck and her legs around his waist. They were probably hungry for each other after such excitement. She could use some alone time with Eiran, herself.

As soon as the door clicked, Belial pried Christy from his torso and held her at a safe distance. He feathered her face and neck with light kisses and smoothed her hair. She clawed at him and he ignored it. He lay them down and quickly fell asleep, deaf to her pleas.

Christy lay there hating him, his soft touches, and his passionless kisses. She didn't want that. She wanted heat, desire, possession. She wanted rough hands holding her thighs apart, teeth at her throat, chest hair scraping against her pebbled nipples, and a rock-hard cock thrusting mercilessly into her. She wanted the harsh animalistic coupling that she knew the Akhkharu could give her, and would, given the chance.

FIVE

Krystal Colbert hung up her phone with a satisfied click. KYTK newsroom was a bustle all around her, everyone unaware that she'd just gotten the information that would make her career. She *would* sit at the news desk as central anchor. After she broke this story, there would be no more "on the scene" reporting of storms or crop conditions or traffic light malfunctions. Krystal had just hit the big time and no one else knew how much things were about to change.

She grabbed her makeup bag and her suit jacket. This would be the last time she applied her own makeup before a shoot. Being an anchor was going to be a dream come true. Everyone would know her name and respect her words.

"Harold, let's go."

Krystal ignored the irritated look her cameraman gave her. She knew he wanted to be called Harry. She didn't want a cameraman named Harry. Harold was much more old school newsman. She longed for the heyday of local news broadcasting, the good old days before cable and the internet took over the news game, when people gathered around their TVs every night at six and ten to find out what was happening in the world. Sure, she was too young to actually remember that time, but she'd studied it.

Tonight, it would be her face that the world watched, her voice that they heard. She had only one informant but that one had just earned his keep. The other news correspondents had their inside sources at the big central Austin police precincts. Hers was very low down, a glorified secretary, at a sheriff's office outside town. They were trying to keep it secret but the sheriff and three of his deputies had disappeared after going to investigate a standard missing person's report.

Whatever was happening at the Sagers' farm was anything but standard and she was going to be the first, maybe only, on the scene. She knew the spies that the other networks had watching the station wouldn't suspect a big story. They would see her in the front seat with Harold and the two of them didn't merit an alarm. Krystal had never had the big story before.

※

CHRISTY WAS relieved to find the Daughters' library was near empty, as usual. Libby was there, as was her husband Leonard. Their living quarters were attached to the bell tower and turret-turned library, so she expected to see them. Their son, Billy, and his mate Minali were thankfully absent. The less people inside the shield when she made it, the better. Belial didn't need to make a circle as the base for her magic here. The library's shape worked for her. Granted, they would have to stay on the ground floor, but the librarian probably had already collected what she wanted to show Christy there.

Libby and Leonard stood staring as the guests made their way toward them. They both had a natural thinness that they had passed on to their son. Libby retained her hardness but Leonard was a little softened with age and he was a bit shorter than she. They were both still very attractive in their sixties. Leonard had an easy contagious smile and his bow tie was always crisply knotted. He was quite tan as a result of being the Daughters' groundskeeper for so many years before handing the position over to Billy. Libby's look was severe, but her attitude was not. She always wore a dress of muted colors, sensible shoes, and the predictable tight bun of gray hair on the top of her head. Though she looked stern, Christy had found her to be an open, happy, supportive surrogate mother type here on the compound.

Belial's pull was not lost on them, but they did their best not to lean into him. Libby hugged Christy, seemingly ignoring Belial, as she led the girl to a study table already piled with books. Belial was excited by the sight of them. "Did you find a book on shield makers?" The sound of his voice only amplified his attractive nature. Leonard took a step closer to the Nephilim before being able to stop himself. He couldn't force his feet to back up, but he reached out and took Libby's hand for support.

"No...well, maybe. I'd 'bout given up on findin' one." Libby's country accent was at odds with her high intelligence. "None a tha regular records say anything about shields or veils. I was fixin' ta admit defeat, but then I remembered these." She gestured to the books on the study table. "These're the oldest in our collection." She handed Christy a pair of white protective gloves and then put some on herself. "We always wear these when dealin' with books so old. The oils in our skin can destroy the fragile paper and ink." Libby said "our" like "are." She got out a mat made of the same cloth and put it on the table. The mat had a softly stuffed roll on either end and when Libby placed an open book on it, they kept the spine from opening all the way.

Christy took a look at the first page. "It's just gibberish." Some of the letters were reversed or squished together and the words were unreadable.

"No, well, yes, it is gibberish. There is no story, and the thing doesn't seem to have much of a point to me, but I can read it. It's just written in middle English. Didn't you ever read Chaucer in school?" Christy shook her head, embarrassed that she had dropped out so early. "No matter," Libby continued. "I can read it to you and see if anything stands out."

Christy fought her desire to sigh at the thought of spending her day cooped up indoors being read to from some old dusty book.

She sat next to Libby as she started reading. Belial moved away a little to lie in the shaft of light coming in the tall thin window. Leonard got his own book, a sci-fi paperback by the look of it, and pulled a chair close to the prostrate Guardian under the ruse of using that same light for reading.

༄

THE MORNING dragged on. Belial and Leonard dozed in their previous, but slightly closer, positions. Libby's voice had lost its enthusiasm and Christy was having a hard time concentrating. "I'm sorry, Libby. My mind wandered off. Can you read that last part again?"

She did, but it made no more sense than anything else. There was something, though. "Do you hear that?"

Libby looked up and furrowed her brow. She shook her head no.

"It's gone now. Go back and read that part again."

"Her children, not Ki, will allow Yahwe to hurt you."

"There it is again. Can't you hear that? It's a humming. It's like…" Could it be as simple as that? Christy wondered.

"The book is shielded, isn't it?" Libby whispered excitedly.

Christy nodded. What could it contain that was so important to be protected so? And how could she see through the shield? She stripped off her gloves and grabbed a notepad and pencil that Libby had placed nearby. She wrote out the words that Libby had said that triggered the vibrations. A simple rearranging gave her the answer she needed. She whispered to the book, "Kiyahwe will not allow you to hurt her children."

Christy looked on as a hidden writing sprung up behind the one Libby had been reading. This one was a form the girl could read. "Dammit," Libby swore. "I was hopin' you could activate it somehow." Christy looked up from the glowing words at Libby. The woman looked deflated.

"You can't see it, can you?"

Libby couldn't, any more than she could hear the vibrations of the shield. This book was for the eyes of shield makers alone. Libby's enthusiasm returned in a flash. "What do you see?"

"There's a hidden text. It says, 'Sister, shield maker, this book is for you. Your first priority is to keep the information contained herein from ever falling into the hands of the one they call Belial Maru.'"

As if hearing his name, even whispered, roused him, Belial stretched and, groaning, stood. Libby quickly took the book and locked it away in a wall safe. Christy knew she could look at it whenever she wanted, but not with Belial looking over her shoulder. She wondered what it would say about him. Maybe it would hold the key to unlocking his passion.

"Is he…preening?" Libby asked quietly.

Christy just nodded. It was more than she could handle, seeing him in all his glory. They watched as he snapped his wings open and shut, shaking them until they were perfect. He ran his hands over his body, removing any invisible dust that had gathered. It made his arm muscles flex in the most pleasing ways. Belial refused to use his camouflage, or maybe he didn't have any. He was what he was, looked exactly as he always had. He didn't wear clothing and he had no hair. Belial was more nude than a person had a right to be.

"Did you locate any books about shielding?" he asked.

Libby's face flushed red as she visibly shook herself out of it. She had been staring at Belial's package. Christy knew because she too had been admiring the soft weight that hung low between his legs. "No, nothing," she lied.

"Come on, Leonard. We have just enough time for a quickie before lunch."

Leonard practically jumped out of his chair. "Yes ma'am." He looked back at Christy and Belial. "Ah, the joys of being retired with the woman I love."

―

NORMALLY CHRISTY did her counseling with Nathalia in the women's center on the far side of the Daughters' compound. Nathalia thought it was good for her to see the results of life with an abuser long-term. Some of the women who took refuge there barely made it out of their relationships alive. It depressed her to see how many of her rescues went right back to their abusers. Since

Nathalia had become a Sinnis, she and Eiran had been making home visits to these abusive men. Most of the time a good scare was enough, but Christy suspected that Nathalia had gone a step further with the unrepentant ones.

Their meeting would not take place there today. Belial still refused to wear any clothes or hide his wings and the sight of a giant winged naked man was more than most of those women could handle, even on a good day. They met in the library. Nathalia was there already, alone, and Christy put up her shield as soon as she and Belial crossed the threshold. Belial sat and pulled Christy into his lap. She closed her eyes and tucked her head into his neck. His smell was addicting. She wanted him so much.

No, this won't work for today. I need to speak with Christy alone. Nathalia spoke to both of them, but Christy couldn't break from her desire trance well enough to answer.

Belial spoke for them both. "Whatever you need to say can be said in front of me. I will not have you whispering about me secretly."

Nathalia smiled at him. She had powers that went mainly unused, but use them she could if the situation demanded it. Though it was the opposite of what his pull made her want, she stared into Belial's eyes and filled his mind with the desire to give the two women privacy. She pushed her thoughts into him. He stood and set Christy down in the seat he'd vacated. He, without any further objection, went as far away as the shield would allow. Christy stared after him, her longing clearly muddying her thoughts. Nathalia then forced Christy to put up a second shield around the two of them. She had drawn a circle around the little sitting area in this section of the library for just such a purpose. Once it was formed, Christy's mind was again her own. She looked at Nathalia, as if waking for the first time in days.

Better? Nathalia asked with a smile.

Christy nodded, closed her eyes, took a deep breath, and let it out slowly. "Yes. I can feel him here but the overwhelming attraction is dulled. When I am with him it is so strong. It's unnatural how helpless I am to resist."

It is anything but unnatural to be attracted to your Nephilim. You should have seen me those first few weeks. You'd hardly have recognized me. Now, let's begin as we always do. How are you, Christy?

They talked, but Christy didn't tell her that her attraction to Belial wasn't right. It did seem unnatural to her and now that she knew she could put another shield around herself while inside the one made for Belial's safety, she planned to use that to gain her sanity back. Around him, she hardly seemed herself. She looked back at her behavior, the way she fawned over him, and knew she had to stop. He got that from everyone. Maybe that was what was holding him back in their relationship. He wanted something different from her. She held out hope that the book could help her get through to him.

"I've been having fantasies about…another, not Belial. I think Hunter may have ruined me for good guys. I can't stand Belial's soft, loving touches. I want dominance and possession. How 'effed up is that?"

There is a difference between rape and aggressive consensual sex. Sometimes when intense things happen to us at key moments in our development, they change us. Things get all twisted together in our minds. For you, love can't be gentle. It needs to be consuming, but your lover must be mindful of your needs. Let me assure you that a Nephilim's first and main desire is to bring pleasure to his Sinnis. Belial will come around. He will figure out what you need and find a way to give it to you. Did you know that Eiran sometimes makes love to me as a woman?

Christy shook her head no.

Yep. It took a while, but he finally figured out what I desired and is happy to give it to me. Of course, there are plenty of times I want him just as he is, and you will be the same. Belial, just like Eiran, has total control over every cell in his body. He can be anything, anyone, you need him to be. He can bring you pleasure like you can't imagine.

"He can and does but…he won't have sex with me. He does… stuff…to me but he won't let me… Goddess, this is so embarrassing…and stupid. I am complaining because he doesn't want to do anything but go down on me. Most girls would be thrilled to have the same problem, but I've never felt more unloved in my life. That doesn't make sense, I know."

So far there were very few Sinnis and so they were not entirely sure of every part of the conversion, but they knew there had to be a blood exchange and sex before the birthmark would take. If there had been no sex, then Christy was unclaimed. Christy was still human. Why would Ini-herit Belial Maru leave her in such a dangerous position? Nathalia wondered. She pulled down the collar of her shirt to show her own birthmark, glowing red just below the surface of her skin, nestled in the hollow of her neck. *You do not wear his mark, then?*

"Belial won't even let me touch it. He says I'm too young." Christy hated that her voice sounded so pouty, so childish. It almost proved him right.

That was odd, indeed, Nathalia thought. There were plenty of Nephilim whose Sinnis were still children. They must wait for years to make their claims, but there was no reason for Ini-herit Belial Maru to suffer and wait. That was another thing bothering Nathalia. Belial was Ini-herit's father's name. Nathalia thought it was curious that Christy would be calling him by it. A Nephilim's birth name was their greatest secret, but he should have felt safe sharing it with his Sinnis, claimed or not.

Your Nephilim knows best. Christy tilted her head and cocked her eyebrow in question. Nathalia laughed silently. She had always been so sexist, thinking of men as work horses and breeding stock to be used by women. That was before. *Weird to hear, coming from me, but I have come to accept that they have great knowledge and wisdom. I know it is hard to stomach the seeming rejection, but it is only for a while. Belial must have his reasons for making you wait. Take heart that you have right of Sinnis to him. Believe me, it is a heady mix, to know that you alone have the privilege to provide prana to such a creature and that his blood is yours.*

SIX

Coffee, having originated in Ethiopia, was a central part of that culture. It was one of the few things Minali held onto in her new American life. Luckily for her, the USA was practically fueled by the stuff, though it was more of an addiction here than the sacred social ritual it was back home.

Their apartment was flooded with the sweet nutty smell of baklava. Billy already associated that scent with the idea and identity of home. Although the treat was not invented in Ethiopia, the people there had adopted it long ago as their own preferred dessert and it was common to finish a meal with it. The smell was intensified by the slightly higher than normal temperature in which they kept their apartment. Minali was used to the heat and felt cold more easily than most. Billy was used to the increasingly hot Texas summers, quite comfortable at whatever temperature Minali chose.

Christy had told him of Belial's shielding needs and Billy had measured and traced an exact circle within the confines of his apartment. It covered all the rooms but didn't extend into his neighbors'. Belial and his wings took up more than half of their living room, so Billy allowed him to get situated comfortably before Minali brought the coffee service in from the kitchen. Neither wanted to risk it being broken since it was one of the few items that she had brought with her from her homeland. It had belonged to her mother's mother, and her mother's grandmother before that.

Shock was clear on Minali's face when she saw Belial sitting on the chair in her parlor. The porcelain coffee pot lid slid from its perch and knocked a matching cup from its saucer home. They both smashed into the hard floor and shattered before Billy could jump to save them. He took the clattering tray from Minali's trembling hands and put it on the table. He ran into the kitchen and came back with the broom and dustpan to find Belial had risen from his seat.

Billy wasn't sure if she was aware of it at all, but Minali was drifting toward the Nephilim. "Belial, Belial, Belial…" she spoke it as if the word held magic and she was both equally afraid of triggering it or losing it. "You're the one who came to me that night. Why didn't you come back when I called for you? I needed you and you ignored me, ignored my pull. No one can ignore my pull." She was shaking her head no now, and tears streamed down her face. This was not going how they had planned, and Billy knew having the Nephilim here was a very bad idea indeed. "How could you? I kept calling, building my pull, feeding it all the extra power collected by the Capacitors until…that monster came instead of you." She had reached him and began to pummel his broad chest with her fists. "You made me…I called…him…he killed… It's my fault they are all dead. It's your fault. I hate you!" Her sobs mixed with screaming until she was barely understandable.

Belial seemed completely unaffected by her fit. He simply, unemotionally, trapped her in his arms and kissed her. The passion grew quickly like a fire in a hay barn. Christy jumped up at the same time as Billy. "Hey! Get your hands off her. You can't come into my home and kiss my mate if she doesn't want you to, and she clearly doesn't." He should have said "didn't" because Minali's anger had melted away. Her eyes were heavily lidded with desire and she traced the lines of Belial's chest where only a few seconds ago she had been hitting him.

"What the hell did you do to her?" Billy pulled Minali back, getting between her and the Nephilim that was so affecting her. He poked his finger at Belial. "Get out of my house. You're not welcome here."

Belial calmly lowered himself to eye level with Billy. Their faces were only centimeters apart when he spoke. "Yes, I am. You would do anything to keep me from leaving." There was the faintest brushing of lips. "You want to please me, don't you?"

Billy nodded, trying to kiss Belial again. "More than anything," he muttered. Belial rewarded him with a deeper kiss and Christy knew something was horribly wrong. Maybe Belial and Minali had a history, maybe a relationship, that made kissing acceptable, but Billy wasn't even bisexual. There was no reason for him to lean into Belial's touch, no reason for him to long for his kisses.

Belial pulled away and told Minali, "Undress."

"Now wait a minute. A kiss is one thing…" Christy shook Billy. She needed him to snap out of it. She needed an ally. She didn't find one.

Belial glared at her, flames in his eyes. He wrapped his hand around Billy's throat and squeezed. Billy made no objection. "You should be glad it does not please me to kill him for mating a woman with the same pull as I." He released Billy and pushed him and Christy back onto the couch. Minali, who was now nude, having completely ignored the exchange, clawed at Belial, much in the same way Christy usually did, like she wanted to tear him apart and devour him.

Belial stroked her body and kissed her into a frenzy before laying her down on the coffee table and kneeling between her knees. Minali moaned and writhed as Belial lifted her ankles, planting her feet on his shoulders. Just before his head dipped low enough to kiss Minali's nether lips, Christy called out, "I claim right of Sinnis. I alone provide you with the prana you require. My blood, my sex, will sustain you as yours will me." Her words sounded more formal than she felt and she wondered where they'd come from. She was desperate and when they jumped into her mind, she had blurted them.

Belial didn't even look her way. His chuckle cut her to the bone. "You have no right to such a claim." His wing flicked out and dragged against her lips, coating them with gold. Her tongue ran across them, gathering his essence. He wrapped her in his wing and tucked her behind him. She no longer cared what happened between Belial and Minali. She was surrounded by him. He must love her. If it pleased him to make love to Minali with his mouth, Christy could no longer think of any reason why he shouldn't do it.

※

BELIAL DIDN'T care where they spent their time as long as there was a circle for Christy's shield. And a mirror. He loved to look at himself in all manner of reflective surfaces, except the antique beaten copper mirrors of the sanctuary. They were used to reflect the sun and moonlight in a warm way that made the statues appear lifelike. Belial said they made him look like someone else and Christy could tell from the way he said it that he didn't care for this other person very much.

Christy spent a lot of time in the library studying the book that only she could read. Whenever she could she threw up a second shield around her, cutting off Belial's pull. It made it possible for her to concentrate. She had Leonard bring in a mirror for Belial. It was heavy with a decorative metalwork frame. Belial didn't notice anything except his beauty. He spent hours amusing himself with his own glorious reflection.

Much of what was hidden in the text was useless to Christy. She tried the techniques, but nothing worked until the day she got a paper cut. The blood gave her an idea and as she read, she knew she'd stumbled on the answer to their tear in the veil. It wasn't difficult, but it relied on having the exact right circumstances, just as opening the tear did.

Nathalia was quick to offer any help she needed and Christy did need assistance. She couldn't do it alone because she needed the three sisters. The Romans had called them the Parcae, the Greeks, Moirai. The prophesies all spoke of how important the three would be, but not what they would be needed for. Nathalia was Ereshkigal, Atropos, Beletseri, and Morta. She was the warrior, the one responsible for cutting the thread of life. She was death. Camilla was Shaushka, Clotho, and Nona. She was the healer, the one responsible for spinning the lifelines. She was birth. Genevieve, toddler-sized though she was, was Ishtar, Lachesis, and Decima. They were not certain what she was to do. In the mythologies she was responsible for deciding a person's fate. She measured the thread. She was supposed to be the mother of all right and proper love. Genevieve was life.

This needed to happen fast. Belial would be exposed while she wove her spell. Also, Christy would have to be in close proximity to the Shinar for the time it took her to cast the gisig. Christy wouldn't have a trial run. She had the Nephilim, the only ones safe from the Shinar, build an archway over the space thinned and weakened in the veil. She needed boundaries for the gisig and it was the best she could think of since the tear was floating in the middle of the room. If it had been on a wall, as Nathalia said the other she knew of was, the arch wouldn't have been necessary. She did all of the prep work she could in a safe place. Some of each of the three sisters' blood had to be mixed with pulverized Shinar bone. Not any bone would do, either; it had to be one that had passed through this exact place.

Christy had worried that this would be an impossible ingredient, but could tell by the way Nathalia blanched when she asked, that the First had access to such a thing. It also told her that Nathalia feared it. Nathalia wouldn't let her touch the fragments of the dagger that had been used by Michael to open that tear in the first place. Nathalia carefully placed the slivers into the mortar that Christy had borrowed from Ingrid, the potion maker. Christy used the pestle to grind down the shards into a fine powder and was surprised to find they were easily crushed. She would have thought the bones of gods to be more durable than that.

Nathalia and Camilla added their blood first and the glowing white powder ate it up. Genevieve went last and left screaming from the little finger prick needed to draw a few drops. It didn't take Christy long to see that something wasn't quite right.

"Maybe Genevieve's too young to be part of this spell." She scrunched up her face. "Maybe she has to be more mature for her blood to work." Christy was guessing. She wished she had some answers for the women who had so changed her life. She wanted to be useful to them.

Nathalia and Camilla looked at each other knowingly, as if they'd had the same thought at the same time. Camilla was never one to speak if there was someone else to do it. Nathalia shared, *Maybe it's because she is unclaimed. She's a Sinnis, but her blood is unchanged. It's still human blood.*

Sam appeared a moment later and Christy knew it was because Nathalia had silently summoned him. *Genevieve is Sam's Sinnis. It will be his blood that joins with hers when she is claimed.* The giant pierced his wrist with his wicked looking incisors and let the blood flow into the mortar until the wound healed. He licked his arm clean as they watched the bloody paste turn from red to black.

"Perfect!" Christy exclaimed. She rushed down to the nursery, which was now stripped of anything that might identify it as such. After she was done, they would wall up the door and windows to this room. They had wanted to fill it with concrete too, but Christy had stopped them. They might need to be able to use the portal in an attack.

Everyone waited outside. Only Christy and Belial, for he would not leave her side, stood inside the room. He would take her from the room if anything she did angered the Shinar or if they made a grab for her. He would not sacrifice her, not even for the good of the rest of the world. He needed her.

Christy had memorized the ancient words, though she had no idea what they meant. They had to be said just right and a translation wouldn't work. Libby said it couldn't be done. They were written in a dead language. No one knew how to pronounce any of it, not positively absolutely. Nathalia's Nephilim, Eiran, had helped. They all spoke the ancient language and even used the words that had no direct modern equivalent, but they had all lived in the modern world and their accents had evolved because of that. Eiran had lived in a cave in the desert from the time it wasn't a dead language until just a few years ago. It was still his native tongue and he easily read the words, practicing with Christy until she had it perfect. He could have translated the words, but had said that it was probably for the best that she didn't know what she was saying. Eiran had forbidden her to say the words in front of Belial.

She would have to say them now, and Belial wasn't going anywhere, but once they were said, they couldn't be unsaid, so she went for it. Incantation spoken, Christy flicked her wrist in a repetitive motion over the mortar filled with black paste. It flew from the stone container to the archway. Each fleck floated, forming a net covering the opening. It wasn't finished. The shield maker's blood, her prana, was needed as the yarn to tie it all together.

She used a pin to prick her pointer finger and thumb on her right hand. Pressing them together and pulling them apart along the face of the gisig, Christy made an angled stitch. When she had covered the whole area, re-stabbing her finger pads as many times as needed to keep the blood flowing, she had to cover it again in the other direction. It made a crisscross pattern that looked very like handwoven material. When she pulled her hand away, the movement sent ripples out to the stone of the arch and floor only to hit it and return back to her.

SEVEN

Christy had done it. She'd sealed the gap in the veil in Genevieve's nursery. Everyone seemed thrilled with her, except Belial. He just looked angry and suspicious. Christy was too exhausted to care. Repairing a tear between two worlds took much more from her than throwing up a shield. This was a thing a goddess had created, that they all expected her, a regular girl, to fix.

Belial got her back to their room, somehow. It took the last ounce of energy Christy had left to put up their personal shield, but she did it. She stood, swaying on her feet, trying to get her shoes off without bending over. Failing, she headed toward the bed. She needed to be near it when she collapsed, shoes or no.

Belial stepped between her and her goal. Fire danced in his eyes. "Where did you learn to do that?" He waited, but the only sound was his heavy angry breathing. "Last week you had no idea how to repair the veil. What happened between then and now?" His last shred of control was destroyed when she raised one shoulder and let it drop but did not speak. He grabbed her by her throat and shook her. "You've met him, haven't you? You've been talking to my brother! Believe me when I tell you that you are never going to see him again. You belong to me."

That energized her slightly. It was more passion than she had ever seen from him. His hand tightened on her throat and her eyes bulged. She clawed at his arm, but she didn't want him to stop. Here it comes, finally, she thought. I will have passion from Belial at last.

Belial's nostrils flared as he smelled her arousal. The look on his face spoke volumes. He was disgusted by her response to his anger. He flung her onto the bed, and she landed face down. Christy imagined him shredding her clothes and plunging himself into her, maybe even taking her in the most taboo of places and the air thickened with her smell. She felt the bed sink under his weight and her hopes were renewed for a second. He climbed on top of her and gripped the waistband of her pants. With a tug, they were gone along with her panties.

She was disappointed when he flipped her onto her back and eased his face, not his cock, between her legs. Her knees fell open and he feasted on her. She cried tears, not of joy, but of frustration as he brought her to orgasm and devoured her prana. He was never going to give her what she needed. He didn't love her. He didn't even care about her beyond her ability to shield him. She wanted him desperately but it was in a way that he was completely unwilling to furnish.

∞

WHEN CHRISTY awoke, Belial was sitting at the foot of the bed. He still looked angry. Even angry he was the most beautiful thing she'd ever seen. "It is the book, isn't it? You found it and I must have it. It will tell me where she lies."

Christy wanted to ask who he was talking about, wanted to feel some jealousy for the woman he obviously felt passion for, wanted to deny the book's existence as it instructed her to do, but she couldn't. She couldn't muster the energy. She had no idea if it was night or day nor how long she'd slept. What she did know was that she needed more rest. She felt like she might never fully recover from her work on the veil. She rolled over and lost consciousness instantly.

The second time she woke up, it was to rough hands lifting her. She didn't fight. She couldn't. She didn't care where he was taking her. She fell asleep in his arms. She may have suckled at his neck and chest, consuming the essence of him from whatever she could. His sweat, his skin, the fairy-like golden dust that covered him was all she could get to, and while she knew it was nothing compared to what his blood would do, it tasted like healing, energy, and sex.

It gave her that little boost she needed and she was awake enough to recognize their surroundings and throw up her shield once they were inside the library.

LIBBY LOOKED up from her work to see Belial enter carrying a half-dressed Christy. The librarian was just finishing up for the night and, with Leonard inside making their dinner, she was alone in the room. She felt the pull of the Nephilim instantly. She stood and came from behind her desk before she could stop herself.

Belial spoke, "She needs the shield maker's book. Bring it to me. We will take it to our room."

Libby hesitated. She knew what the book said about keeping it away from him, but, as always, his voice, no matter his words, intensified his pull. She wanted him like she had never wanted another person or thing in her whole life. She wanted to go to him, give him what he needed. The book was behind her in the safe and that meant to get him what he wanted she had to turn away from him. Impossible.

Belial sighed and set Christy down on a couch. That snapped Libby out of her trance for a second. Christy didn't look good. They knew it would take something from her to seal the gap, but had expected her to heal quickly from her overuse of magic as they all did. That was clearly not happening. The biggest sign that something was amiss with Christy was that she wasn't wearing any makeup. Christy looked worse than she had the day before yesterday. Belial was not only *not* tending to her needs, he was making it worse.

Before she could protest, Belial took Libby into his arms. His skin was hot, his gaze scorching, and it was all for her. Libby drank it in. When he whispered it tickled. "Having the book would please me. You want to please me don't you…?" He paused.

"Libby," she choked out.

"You want to please me don't you, Libby?" he asked again, but hearing her name on his lips undid whatever reservation she had about him. Still, she couldn't bear to leave him, not with him holding her so closely. Libby didn't even realize she was clawing at him. She was just filled with the desire to tear him open and live inside his skin. His breath would be her air, his blood hers. She was content to substitute his kiss for her plan.

He leaned down and gently grazed her lips with his, but that wasn't what she wanted. She grabbed his head and held it against her face. He opened his mouth and she would have climbed inside him from that vantage point if it had been possible. Once she was drunk on his kiss, he easily liberated himself from her grasp.

"Where is the book?" he asked.

She pointed behind her. Belial backed her up until they bumped the wall. He spun her around to face the safe, keeping his body in contact with hers. He rubbed her body through her clothes, his erection pressed against her backside. He took her hand and placed it on the lock. Automatically, she entered the combination code and put her thumb on the pad. It recognized her and, light turning from red to green, hissed open.

There was only one thing inside. Belial pushed Libby away and grabbed the book. He didn't notice nor care that Libby hit the stone floor hard. So drunk was she on him that she didn't notice nor care that her hip broke. Libby just lay there watching as Belial took the book and Christy away. She cried for the loss of his closeness and wondered how she could earn his favor back.

WHAT HAPPENED? Nathalia asked as soon as she got to the library. Camilla and Nanae were kneeling on either side of Libby, who was lying on the floor. Leonard was pacing, but he stopped to answer her question.

"I don't know. I think she's drunk. She's acting like it, but I don't see how it happened." He wrung his hands and looked paler than Nathalia had seen him look before. Not even when he'd had his heart attack had he looked so weak.

Nathalia took Leonard's hand and used her ability to push a feeling of calm into his mind. She pulled him over to the nearest seat. *She's being healed. She will be fine, I promise. Now tell me exactly what you know so I can help you figure this out.* Eiran stood, as usual, like a silent sentinel behind Nathalia.

Leonard took a deep breath and let it out slowly before starting. "I went to get dinner started and Libby was finishing something up here in the library. When she didn't show up at the table when she said she would, I came to tell her dinner was ready. I thought she probably just got caught up in something. I found her right there on the ground, crying."

That makes sense. She's hurt.

"When I asked her, she said she wasn't. She got belligerent when I tried to help her up. She yelled at me to get away from her, that she didn't want me anymore. Then she cried when I turned to go and begged me not to leave her. It's not like her to cry and this wasn't just crying, she was weeping like someone had died. Then she started laughing saying that she would just find another one. I don't know if she was talking about me or what. She was jabbering, just talking crazy. That's when I had the thought she was drunk. She went to get up on her own and screamed in pain. When she fell back down, she hit her head. Camilla heard her screaming and came rushing in. Nanae said she broke her hip."

Nathalia looked around where Libby had landed. There was nothing she could have tripped over, no ladder from which she could have fallen. Nathalia was at a loss. She knew that occasionally the older couple smoked weed, as many of their generation did, but they rarely drank and never to inebriation. If Libby wasn't drunk and there was nothing to trip over or fall from, how had it happened? She looked around again looking for something, anything, she might have missed. Then she noticed the empty safe, its door open.

She pointed. *What does Libby keep in there?*

Leonard looked and shook his head. "I can't keep track. She has those things all over the library. She rotates them out according to what she's working on. I can tell you that is the one she puts her current work in, since it is closest to her desk."

"Leonard," Camilla called. The healer rarely spoke and so when she did everyone listened. He went to her. "We were able to heal it completely. She'll be all right after some rest. Help Nanae get her into bed."

The tiny healer's giant Nephilim of a mate didn't need any help lifting Libby, but Camilla knew the man needed to feel needed. Leonard led the way out of the library and into their attached living quarters.

Did she say anything about what happened?

"Not that made sense. She said he pushed her and took it but… Leonard would never hurt Libby." Camilla rubbed her pregnant belly. She was due again any day now.

I think we have a problem.

∞

ANY WHO *do not submit will be suspect. Banished.* Nathalia spoke to those Nephilim without claimed Sinnis who lived on the compound. There were so many now; Nathalia had no fear of them any longer. They were not men. The Nephilim were less of a threat to humanity now that the time of Sinnis was upon them. Seeing the end of their internal struggle within grasp made them more stable, less prone to transgressions. No one wanted to be imprisoned at the time their Sinnis might come of age. An unclaimed Sinnis would cause quite a stir and could easily get herself killed. Those few who had their Sinnis were not suspect. Their hunger beast was under control, no longer whispering through their blood, calling for violence and destruction. No matter her confidence, something had happened that no mere man could have executed.

Nathalia could have just called them by name and bound them to the earth. Ki would hold them if Nathalia asked. Knowing their names was a gift from the Shinar when they thought she might serve as their chosen one. She did not want to do that. She needed to evaluate them without restrictions on their actions.

Nathalia gestured to Elle, who looked like she was going to be sick. She stepped forward on shaky legs. Elle, the group's Iudex Primo, could read thoughts with a touch of her hand. She now removed the elbow length opera gloves that protected her from the barrage of messy, unwelcome thoughts touching others brought. Elle was hard, physically, and had even less jiggle than a woman of her youth would normally have. She was also hard mentally, but reading even one Nephilim mind was enough to shake her.

Elle moved toward the nearest Nephilim and her movement showed her six pack abs and v-shaped pelvic muscles. Every bit of her was as hard as her arms. Her magical ability was the reason for her ripped appearance. Working out was something she could do alone. No one touched her in the gym. She looked back at Nathalia with the unspoken question, "Do I have to?" in her eyes.

Nathalia spoke only to her, mind to mind, *I am sorry, but I must know if any of these were the one to hurt Libby.*

Elle's asymmetrical yellow hair, that should have made her look masculine but didn't, slid forward and hid one side of her face as she inclined her head in acquiescence. One after another, she laid her hands on the giant half-breeds. Nathalia asked the questions individually so that Elle could get a reading of their unprepared, uncensored response. By the time she was finished, tears rolled down her face and she shivered despite the warm night. These demigods were balls of lustful hunger and searing red anguish in their isolation. Their thoughts burned, snapping across her mind like a bull whip, so real, so tangible that Elle would not have been surprised if she was actually bleeding, physically injured. Their beastly sides were starved and desperate, their human sides in lonely agony. The balance was delicate, but control was sustained. None had done this thing. She shook her head no and left. She needed to eat something nutritious, sleep for a week, fuck with mindless abandon, and connect with a normal human, not in any particular order.

Their relative innocence proven, Nathalia told them her suspicion. There was only one thing this could be if none of the unmated

Nephilim were to blame. *We have reason to believe an Akhkharu has found a way to breach our defenses.*

"I hate to contradict the First, but that is not possible, Ereshkigal." Sharur, whose name literally meant hunter and tracker, spoke up. He called Nathalia by her ancient name as many of the Nephilim did because he had known her in her previous life. He had served her, tracking down those who broke her laws. "Annu would communicate his location to us. With such a gathering of righteous strength, a Justice Circle would be easy. We have held all Akhkharu accountable. Ki held them for Ud's light and their ash imprisoned. We would not show mercy to evil so close to the One. We swore allegiance."

"The prison has more interned there than it has in many years. You have done well." Eiran complimented them. He was the Keeper of the Betrayers, a type of guard for those who had consumed the blood of another Nephilim until the time that their body reformed from the ash and they could be released. He had lived in that prison for thousands of years, doing his duty, waiting for Ereshkigal to return. Now he only had to visit on the new moon, when Annu held no sway. "Nathalia does not question your loyalty." Eiran preferred to call his Sinnis by her current name. Nathalia was his. Ereshkigal had been his brother's Sinnis.

I do not know how it is possible, only that there is some evidence that evil walks amongst us. Nathalia didn't want to believe it either. She knew how these felt about protecting the Daughters. *One of the Daughters was attacked tonight just after sundown.*

Nurzhan Turel disappeared. Mated to Gwyneth, the daughter of Alisha the Peregrinus Primo, but unable to claim her, Turel was sensitive to any threat. He had so much to lose with Gwyneth so young and vulnerable. Gwyneth and Alisha were of his mother's bloodline and they three shared the same ability. Separating one's self from its earthly shell was useful when searching for something hidden or hiding.

Sharur's jaw was tight. "I would know if a betrayer were near."

Nathalia put her hand on Sharur's shoulder. It had the look of a warrior's embrace. She needed Sharur to know that she did not distrust their abilities. *This one is different. Annu is waxing, near full. For a betrayer to expose himself to her, he must have a way to protect himself from her detection. Any able to hide from her could hide from us.*

"Where was the attack?" Sharur asked, his speech more open.

The library, was all she said and Sharur disappeared from under her hand. He had tabalu'd away, most likely to the library to investigate.

"An Akhkharu in the library?" the one known as Jon asked. He was thinner than most Nephilim, with dreadlocks down to the middle of his back.

Yes, Jon. We suspect so. Nathalia knew his name, but respected a Nephilim's right to privacy, especially with their most protected secret. Their true name could be used against them in the wrong hands.

"The woman you asked about, she was injured?" This was from the darkest skinned Nephilim. Many called him Nox, for he was so near perfectly black that he seemed to absorb the light around him. His head was completely bald, as smooth and hairless as the rest of his body. "Fed from?"

No, not that we can tell. She was…influenced. Persuaded to relinquish something of great importance in a way that seems to have come from our kind. She could have said "your kind" but wanted her warriors to know that she counted herself the same as them.

"The library should reek of its presence with the attack so recent. The place is frequented by many, human and Nephilim alike, but I can sense no Akhkharu." Sharur reappeared and spoke without concern for any part of the conversation he might have missed or interrupted.

"I found something," Turel announced. He led the way. "I examined the shield. If an Akhkharu was responsible for an attack it would have to come through it and that would be evident." He stopped in front of an uninteresting bit of grass. They could all feel the shield was near, but it was invisible to them. Just beyond the circle was sporadically well-shaded by wild tree and underbrush growth. Turel pointed. "Just there the shield is different. If an Akhkharu came through it happened here."

How is it different? Nathalia asked, unable to see anything out of order.

"It is thicker."

"Wouldn't it have to be thinner, not thicker, for something unwelcome to come through?" a Nephilim behind Nathalia asked. She didn't see who.

Turel shrugged. "I can only say that it is different. Something came into contact with the shield here, but no other place."

"Perhaps it is like scar tissue. Something unwelcome came through and the shield repaired itself leaving a thickness," Kovu offered. He looked as if he wished he hadn't said anything. Kovu was covered in scars of his own.

Nathalia knew he preferred to stay camouflaged as much as possible to avoid speculation. Even she didn't know where he had gotten them, but it couldn't have been a pleasant experience. With the healing ability of the Nephilim, a scar would have had to nearly result in death. She absentmindedly touched the scar on her own neck. The wound had ruined her vocal cords, taken her voice, and killed her. Eiran's blood had saved her life, but it could not undo the damage nor remove the scar. She had been human at the time. The same wound now with her healing abilities would likely not be visible for more than a day. She wondered why Kovu didn't simply change his shape to cover them.

Nox disrupted her pondering. "I witnessed the shield maker visit this area secretly the other night." His midnight pitch made him a great night watchman. Even creatures with night vision would have difficulty seeing him. "I did not see anyone else, but I must admit I did not stay long. I was…pulled away."

Most of the Nephilim had the decency to look slightly uncomfortable, if not embarrassed. They remembered that night. Once the shield maker had left Belial unprotected, they could scarcely control their beasts' desire for his blood.

"I smell nothing," Sharur admitted. He relied on his senses to track and sniffing was one of the ways he was most successful, though it was not as elementary as what humans thought of as smell.

"The shield maker is conscious of her shield. She feels it. She knows. Can we not simply ask her?" Jon was often quiet but his silence was pensive. When he spoke it was ever reasonable.

I will question Christy, but not just now. She is weak, resting from repairing a tear in the veil. Maybe in a few days I will speak with her. Nathalia hadn't known it would take so much out of Christy when she'd asked the girl to help them. Nathalia had watched as Christy pulled from the lifelines of those around her. Christy had used a majority from herself and Nathalia worried that the shield maker had taken too much. The girl was still human, after all.

The Nephilim stood stunned. A human girl with shielding ability was one thing, but this one had been able to make a gisig, a doorway between this world and that of the Shinar. Earth might actually win the coming battle. If she was weakened by her work, the shield was less protection than usual. They would be extra diligent in their patrols while she recovered. They were not convinced that an Akhkharu had come through, but if it had, it wouldn't happen a second time. It could be their Sinnis hurt next time so next time couldn't be allowed.

EIGHT

"We have a big problem." Maeve started as soon as Nathalia and Eiran came into the office that morning. "Look what Aaron found online this morning." Aaron was there at his laptop, in his pajama bottoms. He looked ashen and Nathalia wondered if being a Levitus was enough to keep him alive under the strain of providing for Maeve's new dietary needs. He did something on his keyboard and a video of a news broadcast came up on the big screen behind him. It didn't take long for Nathalia to realize what had Aaron looking so scared.

An attractive woman in her late twenties holding a microphone sporting the bold blue letters KYTK came on screen. She was standing on a country road, surrounded by a hilly pasture. Two brown cop cars with "County Sheriff" in yellow letters, an all-terrain vehicle, and an old rusty red truck were parked behind her. "This is Krystal Colbert, on-the-scene reporter." She looked a little stiff as the words "on the scene" came from her mouth. "A few days ago, the owner of this farm went missing. His wife, Bonny Sagers, got worried when neither he nor their son came in for supper, but couldn't go looking for them herself as she is recovering from back surgery. She called her neighbor who promised to look for them. He was never heard from again. Bonny called the sheriff's office and was told that normally 48 hours must pass before filing a missing person's report, but since three people had gone missing, these were extenuating circumstances. Sheriff Barton and three of his deputies were dispatched. They too were declared missing."

At this point the cameraman turned and the two started walking. Krystal kept talking. "I found the abandoned vehicles where Mrs. Sagers said I would. What she did not say I would find is that." She pointed to something just beyond a hill. "I am going to keep the camera rolling as we investigate so that you can see exactly what we do, when we do. We have not approached the heatwave-like disturbance in the air that I hope you can see as clearly as we can."

There was a muffled sound. The cameraman was speaking, but because he had no microphone it was hard to make out. Sounded like, "We shouldn't be here, Krystal. Something isn't right."

Krystal looked irritated at the cameraman. "Get a shot of the ground, Harold." He did. There was an invisible line, a rough circle. On the outside the grass was green, on the inside brown, dry and dead. "What happened here?" She stepped into the circle and the ground gave slightly under foot. A puff of dust came up with every step. Harold captured it all. The dust was all that was left of the grass, like ash in the shape of a log that disintegrates as soon as it is touched. Harold spoke again as he put the camera's focus back on the edge. The green grass was, not so slowly, being taken over by the brown. What he said was inaudible.

"Get this." The view was a blur as Harold spun the camera. He was clearly rattled, and his professional cameraman skills were the first thing to go. Krystal was standing next to a pile of deputy's clothing, complete with badge, hat, and gun. She pointed to several more in the brown clearing. Some of them were lying in the shape of people, just minus the body. Krystal whispered, but the mic picked it up, "If this is a practical joke, it is in poor taste."

"Look!" Harold yelled and spun the camera to the center of the circle. There, the heat waves were intensifying. A vertical line made of bright light appeared. It widened, whiting out everything around it for a moment before the camera auto-adjusted. What he said next was clear: "Krystal, don't get any closer to it."

Krystal either didn't hear him or couldn't stop herself. As she advanced toward the light, it pulsed. In a few short breaths, her body disappeared, and her professional suit crumbled on top her sensible pumps. Harold screamed and then the camera fell to the ground, the sleeve of his jacket fluttering down in front of the lens.

"Look familiar?" Maeve asked.

Nathalia stared at the screen where the line of light slowly faded. The Shinar were coming through to this world. That was a tear in the veil and if it was not repaired, and soon, the Shinar would absorb the life within reach and gain the ability to step through. The Nephilim and their Sinnis had to stop that from happening. If they failed, life on earth was history.

∞

NATHALIA AND Eiran landed on the Sagers' farm just seconds before Samsiel and Maeve. They had not tabalu'd as it was only a few short minutes flight from the Daughters compound. Nathalia preferred to travel in a manner that allowed her to retain her clothing and Maeve could not tabalu. They looked around, but the area did not look as it had in the young reporter's video. They could not see the prana-stripped land for all the empty clothing piles. There were now hundreds of abandoned vehicles surrounding the area, and a steady stream of people made their way toward the tear in the veil. Nathalia and Eiran turned to find the tear wasn't a thin line anymore. The opening was almost window-sized and would soon be big enough for the Shinar to step through. Once that happened, it would be too late.

Maeve's focus was on the people, not the opening. A young woman passed near them, her attention on the portal, and Nathalia and Maeve fell into step. The woman was singing a hymn quietly. *Why do you sing?* Nathalia asked her.

"I go to be with the Lord. How could I not sing his praises?" She stopped then and turned to Nathalia. "Is it possible you do not yet know the Savior? There is still time, you know. It is not too late to be taken in the rapture. Praise God, he is not yet done using me. We are here at this moment so that you might know and accept Chr…"

Why would you think this is the rapture? Nathalia interrupted her, not wanting to be witnessed to.

"Look around you. Is it not just as the Bible foretold?"

"The Bible doesn't talk about…never mind." Maeve joined in. She was the expert on this particular brand of crazy. She could argue it for hours and Nathalia had actually seen her win some. "What if I were to tell you that this is not the rapture, those are not angels nor visages of god you see?"

"I would say you were a demon, sent by Satan to gain my soul, or attempt to, one last time. Look at them. They are made of light, just as He is said to be. I feel just like Moses. Is my hair turned gray yet, now that I have looked upon Him?"

No, it hasn't. And just because something is beautiful doesn't mean it is good. Sometimes goodness can be found in the dark.

The woman looked at Nathalia like she was crazy. The Bible spoke often of dark and light and there was no doubt as to which categories good and evil fell into.

Maeve took over again. "This cannot be the returning of Christ. The Bible says the anti-Christ will come first and deceive many. You are falling for it. The anti-Christ has not come yet."

"Why yes, he has. Darkness sits in the White House."

Oh goddess, she thinks President Obama is the anti-Christ! I would love to let her feed herself to the Shinar, be rid of one more racist crazy, but it fuels them and makes them more powerful. What can we do?

Maeve shrugged. "Use your ability, I guess. Send this round home and give us time to get Christy prepared. She did it before; maybe she can close this tear too."

※

"SHE CANNOT. She is not recovered fully. It would kill her, and I need her." Ini-herit Belial stood with his arms crossed over his chest just inside the doorway. Though he was only inches away from Nathalia, she couldn't touch him or Christy from the outside of the small shield. Nathalia could see Christy sleeping on the bed behind him.

She hadn't wanted to ask, but the situation was desperate and getting more dangerous with every minute. Christy was the only shield maker they knew of. Nathalia had asked in every branch of the Daughters, searched every corner and no one had heard of the ability. If Christy couldn't stop this tear from becoming a full-blown portal…well, the thought of empty streets and lifeless wildernesses made Nathalia's sense of urgency outweigh her concern for Christy's health.

Eiran's body pressed against her from behind, giving her strength to question Ini-herit's treatment of his Sinnis. *Give her your blood. She would be healed, made whole, instantly. I can't understand why you are struggling against what is the natural next step. You have found her, now you must claim her and that starts with a blood exchange.*

Ini-herit had grown increasingly angry as her mental tirade had gone on. His nostrils flared. "That would ruin everything we have."

That is ridiculous. It is okay to be frightened. This will be a great change for you, yes, but the key word in that sentence is "great." The bond you'll have with her might be scary at first but…

"I am not afraid. I have lived in fear for more years than you have lived. I am tired. I will not take away her ability with my blood, not to save her life and not to save all life on earth." Ini-herit Belial slammed the door in her face.

Nathalia stood staring at the wood up close. What he said made no sense. Drinking Eiran's blood, being converted, accepting his birthright, had made her ability stronger, not taken it away. Without the blood of her Nephilim, a Sinnis wasn't whole.

She is not his Sinnis. Eiran spoke to her silently. He had heard her thoughts, so solid was their bond that her thoughts were like open conversation with her Nephilim.

She spun to face him, shock in her eyes. It was simple, but she hadn't seen it before. Christy wasn't Ini-herit Belial's Sinnis. That was why he knew that giving her his blood would take her ability. Lilitu, vrykolak, even vitala, the creatures humans became after consuming the blood of a Nephilim or Akhkharu, had none of their powers from their previous lives. If Christy was not his Sinnis, she would be made one of those three, unless he killed her in the process. It was also the reason that he had not shared his true name with her. He had not found his Sinnis; his name could still be used against him.

She wrapped herself around Eiran. *Take us back to the site. I have to send them away again.* They both knew she couldn't do it forever. It was only a temporary fix, but that was better than doing nothing. Then they had to decide about Ini-herit Belial. No Nephilim had ever laid claim to a woman that wasn't his Sinnis. He couldn't keep her from fulfilling her destiny. Christy was the answer to everything and Belial wouldn't be allowed to keep her tucked away for his use only.

※

NATHALIA HAD dispensed with the monsters, both Akhkharu and their dark children, that followed him over the long years. Ini-herit Belial could not use them as he wanted to. He knew his brother was still alive. His brother would try to take Christy from him if given the chance. Her shield was the only thing keeping his brother away and that would fall as soon as she touched it.

Ini-herit had never so blatantly spread his allure over a place. He found he quite enjoyed it now. He had chosen the place not completely at random. It was one of the Daughters' compounds of the most northern part of this continent. They had no Nephilim to protect them, all Guardians having gathered in the heart of independent land. He knew his brother had carried on an affair with one of the women there ages ago and would still feel a sense of duty to them. The women were most accommodating; he was scarcely induced to use his kiss to subdue any of them.

He left a few of those he knew to have communications talents unaffected by his pull. He covered the place with his smell. It would not be long before the creatures of power were drawn to this place and it would only be a matter of time before his brother would come to their rescue. Then Ini-herit would be free to take Christy wherever he needed.

He hoped he would not need her for much longer, but wouldn't risk losing her until he was sure he was done with her. If he could find and destroy his mother's body, he would be free of his power, his curse. He gave no second thought to what it would cost his brother or humanity. He had no Sinnis. He did not care if the whole human race was wiped out. He would live in peace.

He left them in a frenzy as quickly as he had appeared. No one could track a Nephilim through the mother earth. He reformed himself in the cramped room Christy called home and was relieved to find her still unconscious, the shield around her room still intact. Now he waited.

∞

INI-HERIT KISSED Christy awake. He poured on the desire to please him at any cost. He filled her with it. His hands traced her body, igniting a spark of energy in her wherever they touched. Christy opened her mouth wanting more than anything for the passion to build. She clutched at his arms and shoulders, working her way up to his head. She laced her fingers behind him, clamping him against her.

He put all his weight on her, and she moaned into his mouth at the deliciousness of that pressure, that helpless trapped feeling. He rocked his hips and his hard length slid against her mound. Another moan escaped her as he humped, showing her how passionate he could be if he wanted, if she pleased him.

Then he was gone. She sat up quickly and watched as he brought the book to her. He smiled and pointed to it. "Say the words, show the text to me."

All she knew was that she would do anything for him. The book said to protect the information inside from Belial, but if he wanted to know, she would tell him. She didn't owe the author any allegiance. "Kiyahwe will not allow you to hurt her children." Her voice was scratchy from disuse. The text changed and the secondary words moved to the front. They seemed to hover over the obvious words. She turned to him expectantly.

He shook his head at her. He couldn't see them. "You will have to read to me." She started, but he stopped her. "I do not care about repairing the veil nor can I learn to make a shield. Look for any information about a woman named Gazbiyya."

The book sputtered and spit sparks. Belial stepped back, as far away from the book as the shield and walls of their room would allow. The book settled down and Christy watched as the words changed yet again. "Yes, here it is. Wait." She furrowed her brow as she read silently.

"What does it say?" he demanded.

She shook her head. Belial rubbed his forehead with one hand and sighed. He looked almost as tired as she. He took a step toward her and then stretched his wings out as far as the room size would permit. Pulling himself to his full height, he stood before Christy in all his glory. A squeak escaped her lips, almost as if she were in pain trying to keep something that he wanted from him.

"It says not to tell you where to find her. Who is she and would you really destroy her if you could?"

He never said a word. He gave no weight to her questions. He didn't want to use the kiss on her again so soon. His kiss was his only weapon and it was the apex of his ability. He hated using it but had decided, if he had to just one last time in order to turn off his power supply, he would when Christy abruptly started speaking.

She read, "Protect, with your life if need be, the knowledge that the body of Gazbiyya, mother of Ini-herit and Imendand Belial Maru, can be found in a cave on Mount Gish near the Abey River." She looked up at him, tears in her eyes from being unable to stop herself from betraying the secret to Belial.

"I cannot believe it. I have been to Gish Abey and never once suspected. Before night falls I will be at peace, my mother's curse lifted."

"Gish Abey. Isn't that where Minali is from? In Ethiopia? You won't be there by tonight. It's probably 14 hours of plane ride." He could have tabalu'd, but to do that with her he would have to convert her, which he had already demonstrated he was unwilling to do. Unless he couldn't tabalu…but that couldn't be. All Nephilim could tabalu. Only Akhkharu could not.

Belial scooped her up and leaped from the window. "I fly much faster." The book fell to the ground, forgotten.

NINE

Nathalia felt the pull and acted on it before she recognized it. She ran, finding herself in the courtyard instantly. Minali was waiting there. "Nathalia," the woman didn't even look when addressing her. Minali's eyes were locked on a figure standing near the shield's edge. She pointed and Nathalia looked.

There stood Billy in vrykolak form in a small area that was shaded when the sun was this low. This was very odd behavior indeed. She wondered what was wrong with him that he would show his beast in broad daylight so close to the road where any unsuspecting human could take him for a giant wolf monster. It was forbidden. *What happened?*

They were walking the grounds before joining his parents for dinner. Libby was feeling much better and, having healed quickly with Camilla and Nanae's aid, wanted them over for her famous strawberry shortcake. "Billy was making rounds, deciding what needs doing tomorrow. He stopped and sniffed the air. He told me to stay in the sun and to run to safety. He said to send for you and then he exploded in fur. It was the fastest change I've ever seen him do."

Nathalia watched as three vrykolak jumped over the stone wall and landed in the shade inside where the shield should have been. The Daughters definitely had a problem. The shield was down and sunset was only an hour away. Right now, the evil beasts were restricted to the shadows, but as soon as the sun was down, they would have free reign and could attack from any and every angle.

Get everyone inside, Minali. Use your power to send every available Nephilim to me, Maeve and Izzy too. Maeve wasn't a Sinnis, but Izzy had proven that Lilitu were damned near as immortal as Nephilim. If there was an invasion of Akhkharu and their dark children, Nathalia would need all the help she could get. This was going to be a long night.

She wondered why Christy had let the shield drop and sent out a word to the girl. It was no use. Christy was no longer on the grounds. Belial had taken her. He was the one to hurt Libby too, she was sure of that now. How had he fooled them? she wondered. Was he an Akhkharu? Only a monster would choose his own comfort over the safety of the One. Christy was in danger, but the Daughters didn't have the shield to protect them and if forced to choose, there was no contest for Nathalia. The needs of the many always came before the needs of one, unless that one was the One. Then no number of lives were more valuable.

Eiran moved, brushing against her. They walked together to stand with Billy facing the threat. He humphed in recognition of their arrival but never took his gaze from the enemy. His claws extended, gouging the ground. Billy was ready to fight, ready to die to protect them all. Nathalia reached out to pet him but thought better of it. Instead she rubbed her shoulder along his. Even on all fours he was almost as tall as she in this form. He acknowledged her. They were in this together.

∞

THE FLIGHT had been invigorating at first, but eventually Christy's exhaustion had won out. She had only a few moments of lucidity throughout the whole trip. It was torture for Belial to hold her so close yet keep from her what she deeply needed. She wanted to feel outrage, but that emotion took much too much energy.

At least Belial understood the limits to her strength and didn't put her down when he landed. He stood there in what Christy assumed had been a courtyard before whatever catastrophe that destroyed it had hit. So this was Gish Abey, she thought. Minali and she were Libby's surrogate daughters, making them sisters of a sort. While Christy knew something horrible had happened to the place in that part of the world where the Daughters called home, Minali hadn't said anything about this.

It looked like a bomb had gone off and no one had bothered to repair or rebuild. The building itself was nearly destroyed and rubble piles littered the once well-manicured lawn. Plant life was trying to take it back over in most places, but the ground was sprinkled with spots that looked like Christy felt. They were dark and dead, scorched as if the fire had happened only yesterday. The blackened areas were spotted with bits of bone, bleached white by exposure to the sun. It was only when Belial carried her past one, close enough for her to see, that she realized these were human remains. Hollow eye sockets stared up at her from fractured skulls.

Christy looked away, focusing on the sacred spring she could see in the distance. It was like an island in the sea of death she now found herself in. Gish Abey was the town nearest to the Daughters of Women compound. Their actual land lay near the three natural springs that fed the Blue Nile. Those springs were considered holy by pagans and Christians alike and were known to possess healing powers. The Christians claimed it, but Nathalia had told Christy it was because of the Sister's sacred burial grounds.

Magically charged women granted special properties to the land where their bodies were buried. In Texas they had a sacred ficus grove. Those trees bloomed and produced figs year-round from the secret in that soil. The fruit had healing and other desirable powers. Here, the bodies blessed the spring water.

Belial shifted her and she found herself cocooned in his wings. It was beyond pleasant and she slipped right back into unconsciousness. When she woke, it was a shock that Belial had tied her wrists together with rough and sturdy rope. He stood her up on her own two feet and walked away.

"You can't leave me here like this." Christy pulled at the chains that threaded between her rope tied hands and held her bolted to the ceiling. They didn't give. She was tethered without enough room to even sit down on the ground. Her hands were forced up at shoulder height.

"I will only be gone for a moment. What I have to do will take very little time." When it was done, Belial wouldn't need Christy anymore, but until he was sure, he didn't want to chance her getting away or getting somewhere with a circle she could use to set up her shield. He needed her until he didn't.

She paused, taking stock. "My legs are ready to give out. Belial, I am so tired."

An irritated gust of breath Belial didn't even try to hide escaped and he left the room. He came back with a simple wooden chair that had a rattan woven seat. He put it under her so she could sit, but the position forced her arms straight up. Now she had a choice. If her legs got tired, she sat. When her arms were aching, she could stand and get relief for them.

"I will be right back." With that, Belial was gone.

IN AUSTIN, the sun had gone down hours ago and the dark vrykolak had not advanced. They had, however, spread out and more had joined them. Their number totaled a dozen and Nathalia wondered if they were all from the same pack. They weren't doing anything. Even so, she was glad the Nephilim outnumbered them, even if it was by only a little.

"NOOOOO!" The anguished wail made them all flinch. The vrykolak finally moved. They howled and growled. Some of them tossed their heads as if in agony and some clawed at their ears with their paws, as if the sound was hurting from inside their minds.

Nathalia looked to Billy. *What's happening?* She spoke only to him. He, never taking his eyes off the vrykolak in front of him, shrugged. Whatever it was, he was unable to feel it. It wasn't a vrykolak thing, it was a pack thing.

A familiar sound broke her train of thought. She looked up to the sky to locate the source of the flapping wings, but the darkness kept the flier hidden. She felt the rush of wind on her skin before two glowing red eyes appeared before her. The Akhkharu was made of darkness. A wall of muscle and hair hovered in front of her, its tattered and torn black wings keeping it from touching the earth. The position also kept Nathalia from being able to bind it to the earth and trap it. To bind it, in addition to its contact with the earth, she would need its birth name. She knew the secret name of every Nephilim ever born, but this one was a mystery. Even after its betrayal and transformation into Akhkharu she should have been able to identify it.

Who are you? she demanded. She broadcasted the desire to tell the truth. She was uncomfortable with the weakened position she now found herself in.

He only laughed, the sound scraping at her mind like a cheese grater against the skin. Nathalia rushed forward and took a swing with her short sword arm. Something as simple as a nick in his skin would slice through his silver thread of life. It would kill him and his prana would gather in her, filling Eiran's birthstone. He didn't even dodge but her blow bounced off him as if he was wearing armor.

"I have no time for this. I seek the shield maker. She is mine. I can smell my brother's scent mixed with hers. Where did he take her?"

Nathalia shook her head. *I don't know.* She was confused by her deep desire to help the Akhkharu, but only for a moment. Then she connected it. If this beast was Ini-herit Belial Maru's brother, then they shared the same ability. It was beguiling her with its allure. *If I did, I wouldn't tell you.*

"Yes, you would," it argued.

I've had your brother housed here for a while and I can resist him.

"No, you can't. He's had the shield maker blocking for him." The Akhkharu drew himself up, growing to his full, gargantuan size. It was truly the thing nightmares were made of. Even so, Nathalia felt drawn to him. "His power is nothing compared to mine. My brother has spent his life running from his ability while I have spent my none too short life building and harnessing mine."

Nathalia hadn't felt herself move, but realized she was now standing close enough to touch him. She wanted more than anything to do that. She put her hand on his rough hairy chest, his leathery arm. She looked up into his face, an action she, at over six feet tall, was unaccustomed to, and he laughed again. He gestured that she should look down. When she did, she saw his claw extended, a hair's breadth away from her abdomen. He would gut her if she breathed too deeply.

"I could cause you to impale yourself. You would go gratefully to your death if that was what I wanted." He shook his head. "You are lucky that is not my desire. Tell me of the shield maker and my brother." The smallest of details could tell him where they had gone. Ini-herit had stolen shield makers from Imendand before; he would die or kill Ini-herit before he let that happen to this one. She was his.

Christy just fixed a tear in the veil.

The Akhkharu growled. She should not have attempted that alone. As a human she would have had to use her own thread of life to stitch up the veil. "She is not well, then."

No, but we can't understand why. None of us are weakened by using our abilities.

"Her ability is shield making. The veil is not a shield and repairing it is something only I or my father can accomplish. The tear must not have been severe or it would have killed her to attempt. How bad is she?" His brother would not have been prepared for the damage repairing the veil would do to her. He would be desperate now that she seemed so weak and fragile.

I don't know; Belial won't let anyone near her. When I went to see if she could do it again, Belial lost it and I realized she was not his Sinnis.

At this the Akhkharu roared in her face, the sound causing her ears to ring and the volume of air blowing her hair back. Even that contact made her ache for more. She wished he would devour her so that she could experience the peace of providing for him and the warmth of being one with him. He did not touch her. With one down sweep of his wings, he was gone into the night.

Imendand knew where they had gone. If the shield maker knew how to repair the veil, she had read the book. If his brother had influence over her and knew she had the book, he would go after their mother's body. Imendand knew where they were going. The book had told them where to find Gazbiyya. He had found the book tossed haphazardly on the ground in the room that so smelled of his Sinnis and brother. He had taken a moment to fix it, carefully laying it on the bed. He had lost it for ages, trusted its safety with the Daughters. Now it had done its job. Belial would spring the trap and Christy would finally belong to Imendand.

Nathalia leaped as if to take off after him. When her feet hit the ground, the spell was broken. She looked around her then to find the Nephilim embroiled in a battle with the vrykolak. Had they been fighting the whole time she had been talking to their maker, or had it just started? she wondered. They seemed to be holding their own and she called out, *Eiran! Quickly, we must follow him!*

Eiran could not break from the fight he was in but looked at her. His look was odd, as if she were talking crazy. In his moment of distraction, the vrykolak he was fighting got the upper hand. The werewolf did not take the kill shot, even though Eiran's neck was exposed. It just showed Eiran that it could have won, and then backed off, waiting for another attack. Eiran had not seen the Akhkharu, Nathalia realized. The monster's camouflage was enhanced by his shielding. That creature was exceedingly dangerous and would be near impossible to find if it wished to remain hidden.

Just then, one of the werewolves broke free of the melee and rushed toward her. They tumbled together in a heap. Nathalia managed to extricate herself without getting caught by the snapping jaws, but she couldn't touch the monster with her sword hand. She did connect with her fist. It made contact with the beast's muzzle with a satisfying crunch. The vrykolak yelped and shook its head, trying to shake off the pain, before straightening up. It quickly recovered and prepared for the next attack.

TEN

Her savior is here. He is a dream come true, a beautiful golden god. Her god. She doesn't have to worry anymore. Nothing bad will ever befall her now that he is here. His face is the definition of beauty, the kind that incites pure unquestioned devotion. His body chiseled and superhumanly masculine in the way only a god's can be. Just looking at him pleases her. It is an honor to look upon his magnificence.

He touches her body and she ignites, pleasure spreading with every drag of his fingertips. Her cheek, chest, arms and stomach all tingle in response. She feels a warmth on her cheek and her god laughs. The shivers start in her core, due to pleasure she thinks, then turn to trembling. She is afraid.

She looks at her god, sees him bring his hand from her to his mouth. He licks the thick dark liquid there and smiles at her with sharp aggressive teeth. Blood. But where did it come from? she wonders. Tingles turn to burning, pleasure turns to pain. Looking down, she sees that he has sliced her skin with every drag she thought was tender. Not fingertips, but claws caress her flesh.

She looks back at her god, the question, Why? clear on her face. She finds him changed. The face that stares back at her is not her god, but a monster. His face is beastly, filled with malice and covered with hair. His eyes glow red, fire inside them threatens to consume her.

The answer to her unspoken question comes. "Because you are mine." The words are innocent enough, but the delivery is a clear threat. He opens his mouth, wider than any creature's should, slowly to allow the fear of his bite to grow. He moves so fast that she doesn't see but feels his shark-like mouth clamp on her throat.

She screams, but it is cut off in a gargle. She is drowning in blood.

Jolie sat up in bed. She was sticky with cold sweat, her hair plastered to her face. She thought about her dream, prophetic for sure. She wondered who the girl had been. Jolie saw from her eyes, but since there had been nothing around them, no setting nor background, she could find no reflection to tell her who this horrible fate belonged to.

She grabbed for the dream journal she kept by her bed, but it wasn't there. Silently cursing, she rolled out of the air mattress onto the carpet of Marci and Tank's spare empty bedroom. Jolie, for the first time ever, was considering leaving the Daughters. Jolie's cousin, Marci, and Tank had left with their baby a while ago. JD had agreed to take Juliet and Jolie to visit and now seemed a good time.

Jolie dug through their luggage for a minute before giving up. JD had packed. She wouldn't disturb his adorable, quiet snoring for this. He could find it tomorrow and record her dream. It won't matter anyway, she thought as she crawled back into bed. The girl in her dream could be any of the Daughters or maybe all of them. She feared it was the fate of them all, that the dream was warning of the dangers of trusting the Nephilim. Jolie had voiced her doubts before, but Maeve and Nathalia refused to see the danger of aligning themselves with the half-breeds. She could call in and report tomorrow, or maybe the next day. What harm would a few hours wait do? It wasn't as if the Daughters would listen to logic when it came to the Nephilim.

∞

NATHALIA'S SWORD arm should have been dripping, coated with enemy blood, her birthmark overflowing with collected prana after an entire night of fighting, but it wasn't. Hours the Nephilim had battled the vrykolak and as far as she could tell neither side had suffered any injuries, much less fatalities. There was only exhaustion: no progression, no ebb and flow, no tide of battle. The vrykolak only broke away from their circling when a Nephilim attempted to leave or back out of the fight. This was not a battle; this was a stall tactic and they had all fallen for it. What were the vrykolak keeping them from? And how in the name of Ki were the werewolves avoiding injury?

Sure, they were taking punches, but no sharp edge had pierced their flesh. None of the vrykolak were going in for the kill strikes either. They were wrestling, grappling, and snapping but either they were very bad fighters or they were coming up just short enough with every blow that none made contact.

The vrykolak were not attacking. This was a spar. Nathalia looked out over her men and only a few were fighting in their true forms. Most were not glowing, did not have their wings exposed, and were not giants. An attack on Nephilim would result in their true forms being forced out. It was a kind of intimidation factor that worked well in the ancient times. It struck fear in any who wished them harm. If they were not in their true forms, then there was no real danger.

Stop! she commanded them all. The Nephilim obeyed, disentangling themselves from the fighting. The vrykolak stopped with them. The beasts sat back on their haunches and watched, panting.

They stood, two lines facing each other. Then as one, the vrykolak turned their heads to the side, one ear up and the other down, as if listening to the same thing. Nathalia could hear nothing. They howled and, turning from the main building, ran away. *This could be a ploy to draw us away from the One. Stay and protect the compound.* Nathalia gave her orders to the other Nephilim. She and Eiran gave chase. It was more than curiosity. Wherever these things were going, the Nephilim needed to know. Their lair could have evidence of their crimes or could be the home of their maker. There might be human casualties.

They had fought all night and Nathalia had never been more thankful that Ud's light would crest the horizon within the next few hours. This pack might be damned near unbeatable in a fight, but if they were of the night, the sun would burn them. All she and Eiran would have to do would be to drag them into its cleansing light.

Nathalia recognized the direction they were headed, though they ran faster than the human eye could see. The vrykolak weren't headed to their home. They formed a perimeter around the ever-increasing tear in the veil. It had grown since the last time Nathalia had seen it, but not by too much. Her mental push to keep people away had worked on everyone within the radius she could reach, but people were clearly coming in from further away, having heard of the phenomenon.

The night had eased the flow of people, but the tear was more of a gap now, almost door-sized. The view was magnificent. The Shinar, visible in the gap, more than glowed; they were made of light and their brightness shone out into the evening sky like a second sun. The werewolves, silhouetted against the light, were a frightening sight. They were enough to cause pause in the humans attempting to cross the boundary.

One man and woman with a group of young girls were pressing forward, though. The vrykolak blocked his path and their growls and roars had the little girls screaming. The man got angry when the girls froze, clutching one another. "I warned you about the trials that would face us. Do not be afraid; these demons cannot touch us," he yelled at them. The woman, their mother, was shaking her head no at him. She would not move forward.

Her children clutched at her skirts. Their dresses, all homemade, matched in pattern and simplicity, but were in various stages of wear. The youngest wore the most ragged, obviously handed down from the older. The father struck the mother with a backhand to the cheek and wrenched a toddler from her hands. "You would damn our children to hell, banishing them from God's light because you are weak of heart. This is why He saw fit to make man the head of the household."

He carried the screaming child toward the line of vrykolak. They did indeed look as anyone would imagine hell hounds. They growled and roared at him, but his steps were steady. He was proud of his unflinching bravery. They were warning the man but when it was apparent that he would not heed them, they escalated from threats to action. One vrykolak locked his jaw around the man's leg on the side where he held the girl. Another gripped him at the shoulder on the other side.

They tore the man apart rather than let him through their line. The man's screams echoed throughout the field. The toddler dropped to the ground. Nathalia stepped in then. There was nothing she could do for the man, but she stopped the mother from rushing forward. That family needed at least one adult alive to take care of them. They all watched as a vrykolak lifted the toddler by the back of her dress, like it would a pup by the scruff of its neck, and carried her over the mangled mess that had been her father toward the huddled weeping group.

It dropped the child near her siblings, completely unharmed, though probably traumatized. It turned to return to its pack and one of the older daughters reached out and stroked its fur and it froze. The mother gasped but when no attack followed, the other sisters petted it too. It accepted this thanks, even licking the face of a small girl brave enough to get close to its head. When it had joined its brethren and taken a chunk of flesh from the dead man, it took its place in line.

Go home and do not come back. Be glad that your family survived. Nathalia helped to herd them back toward the road where their car must be parked. They must be in a large van to fit so many people.

"We can't. I...I am not allowed to drive. He kept the keys. They must be in his pocket still. I don't even know how to get home."

The woman was clearly not ready to be head of this house. Nathalia could see the bruises, both newly blue and old healing yellow, peeking from below the edge of her sleeve. Some of the girls had them too, especially the older ones. Damn that man, she thought. He deserved what he got.

Eiran, always a silent mover, appeared behind Nathalia with the keys. She took them before anyone could see they were sticky with blood. She moved her mouth when she spoke so that they didn't notice the sound wasn't real. *Come with me. I can drive. I will take you to a safe place where you can stay as long as you need. I can offer you free room and board and if you should want, at a later date, a way to be independent.*

Her offer was accepted gratefully by the mother but mostly ignored by the children, who were whispering to each other and staring at Eiran. He kissed Nathalia on the temple and spoke only to her, *Get them to safety. I will stay here and make sure this does not get out of hand.*

The large group of females started their walk and a girl of about eight years old put her hand in Nathalia's. "Is your boyfriend an angel?" she asked. When Nathalia just looked at her, she pressed, "He has wings." Eiran was not showing his wings and Nathalia wondered, now just how did she see them?

CHRISTY WAS fairly certain she was going to die there in that horrible place. It was already stained with such gruesome death that no one would even notice hers. She wished she had some makeup on. It was a silly thing to worry about with death so immanent, but if she were going to die, she at least wanted to look good. Belial wasn't coming back; she was sure. High noon had gone by and she'd dozed. The ache in her arms had passed into blessed numbness around supper time. She'd managed to stay awake for hours into the darkness. Her fear-induced adrenaline making her jump at every sound. But eventually her exhaustion won out.

She knew there had to be people living nearby. This area of Africa was one of its most densely populated. But she dared not call out. Yelling in the night was an unacceptable risk for the possibility of rescue. She didn't want to tempt the approach of any creatures of the night. Tied as she was, she knew she would appear as an enticing morsel to vampires, werewolves, and their makers, Akhkharu. She planned to scream her head off once the sun rose.

Her head snapped up, at what she wasn't sure, and the movement pinched a nerve in her neck. The stinging burn traveled quickly from between her shoulder blades, up her spine to the base of her skull and covered her head with pain. Her vision whited out for a second with the intense sensation. When her sight recovered, a monster stood on the edge of the shadows, its silhouette highlighted by star and moonlight. Her monster, the Akhkharu that filled her with such dread and desire, had come for her.

Christy jumped up, the sound of her chair tipping over and clattering away startling her further. Damn Belial, she though, for leaving me here without even a circle to use for a shield. She couldn't even defend herself for the short time it was going to take the sun to break over the mountains. She was happy to see the horizon was lightening, even if it was only a small bit.

Her legs gave out after only a few seconds of use, but before all her weight tugged on her raw but numb wrists, he was there. With an arm around her waist, he lifted her off the ground, his warmth on her back. "Belial," was all she had the strength to say. He had come back for her after all. The Akhkharu was gone, probably too scared by one single Nephilim to risk injury, even for a tempting taste.

"You may call me Imendand."

Christy wept. He finally trusted her enough to give her his true name. It was finally happening. She felt his breath on her neck and knew this was the moment she'd been waiting for. She dropped her head to the other side, offering her blood to him. He growled and the sound shot straight to her womb. She clenched her thighs together and rubbed her backside against his hard length.

He tugged the wide strap of her tank top to the side for unobstructed access to her shoulder and neck. His kisses were laced with nips of his teeth and the anticipation of his bite grew. Her nipples grew hard, and he must have noticed their peaks poking through the thin material of her blouse because the hand that wasn't holding her off the ground was on them at once. He grasped at them, roughly, and soon the cotton was too much to bear. Christy was thrilled to be touched and hopefully taken in such a manner.

She was suddenly very aware of how little there was between them. He had dressed her in only a tank top and silky skirt before taking off to bring her here. She didn't even have a bra or panties. He lifted the bottom of her tank so that it rested above her breasts, exploring every inch of newly exposed skin possessively. It was such a difference from the soft tender caresses Belial had used before and the change was welcome. She felt totally helpless and out of control and she loved it.

He slid his free hand down off her chest, over her ribcage, down her thigh, and under the hem of her skirt. The scorching heat of his touch branded her as his and sent a rush of liquid straight to her core. Those fingers found their goal, slipping in between her folds. She wasn't embarrassed that it had taken so little to get her so wet. She had been denied what she really wanted for so long; it was like their last weeks together had been extended foreplay. She was done with that. She wanted to be bitten and fucked, both fairly roughly.

He pinched and tugged at her clit until she was writhing in his arms. He spread her labia with thumb and forefinger and began to rub that swollen tender nodule with his pointer. His finger moved faster than any man's and she went from bucking and panting to frozen, holding her breath, on the cusp of an impossibly immense orgasm. Her sudden quiet, her prey-like stillness, like a rabbit trying to lull its captor into thinking it was dead so that it would have the chance to get away, must have triggered the beast in him because this was the moment he bit.

His super sharp teeth slid through her flesh like a hot knife in butter. The pain was sharp, and Christy gasped, but it was immediately replaced with a dull ache that centered deep inside her. His first pull, first draw on her blood brought on her climax. If it was even possible, it seemed that she had two at once. One in the normal way, from the normal place, and the other coming from the connection between her neck and his mouth. There was no slow build, just sudden eruption. Her muscle contractions bordered on violent. She was both weightless and heavy.

She was still reeling, her orgasm going strong, when he reached up and tore her shackles from their connection in the ceiling. He must have shielded her from the falling debris because not a speck of dust hit her. He carried her from inside to out, and once there, he placed her on her hands and knees in the cool dewy grass. Only then did he stop drinking from her.

This position sent the blood rushing back into her arms and she grimaced at the tingling pain. Even that and the discomfort of being bound all night was sweet sensation that added to the experience. She wondered now if this was all part of Belial's plan. She chastised herself for not using his real name, even in her mind. She used it now as her penance. "Imendand, please."

He growled again, this time louder, and said, "Beg me again, little shield maker. Tell me you are mine to do with what I want, and I will give you what you need. I would never deny my Sinnis her desires."

He hadn't asked her what she wanted. He had commanded her to surrender herself to his whim so that he could please her. It was exactly the thing to say. She lowered herself to her elbows, dropped her head to rest in the moist grass. This elevated her ass and she spread her knees as far as they would go to accentuate the point. "Please, Imendand. I'm begging you to take me. I'm yours. This body is for your pleasure alone."

He pushed her skirt up to her waist, exposing her butt. He rubbed the rounded meat with his hand and gave each side a shake and tap. Her admission, her surrender, had left her limp, without resistance. "In every circumstance, in every way imaginable and even those not thought of yet, you are mine."

It was not a question, but still she answered, "Yes, Imendand."

She quivered, aching, in the night air. With his knees between hers, he rubbed the smooth head of his cock over her blooming opening. She moaned and pushed back. Quickly she found her hips held still with a tight grip of his hands. When he knew she was again acceptant of her fate and lack of choice, he released her hips. With one hand heavy on the small of her back, he went back to gathering her lubrication on his erection.

"Do not move." He slipped forward and the ridge of the head of his dick bumped across her oversensitive clitoris. She didn't jump this time. "Good." He moved his hand from her back to front to fondle her breasts and then moved on to her pussy. "Here, you are mine."

His finger was larger than some cocks she'd had in her, and she let out a sigh. "Yes."

The head of his dick smoothed over her rear entrance and she tried to relax, knowing that he wanted her submission. "And when, not if, I decide to take you here?"

She thought about Imendand pushing himself past her sphincter, holding her down, pressing himself further and further inside her nearly made her come again. She managed to force out the words, "If it pleases you, Imendand, it pleases me. I am yours in every way, if you will have me."

He flipped her onto her back. She was highlighted in the moonlight but he was silhouetted above her. The stone, his birthmark, glowed red in the darkness. Though she could not see it, she felt his gaze absorbing every detail of her naked form. Slicing through the rough rope that still bound her wrists, he ordered her, "Hold your legs wide open for me."

She grimaced at the sting of the air on her raw wrists but she did as he said. She used her hands, palms against her inner thighs, to push her already spread knees flat against the ground. He noticed her discomfort and remedied it. He pricked the thumb and first finger on each of his hands on his elongated teeth. He spread the balm-like blood over her lacerated skin and it was instantly relieved.

"Spread yourself for me." His voice was little more than a growl now, but she understood him. She followed his order because it turned her on just as much as it pleased him. She used her fingers to separate her already swollen outer and inner lips, showing her glistening opening.

Without preamble, he buried himself inside her. She cried out loudly and almost missed his roar. It was almost like a lion's. It was heaven to be filled after so long without. He lowered himself so that his weight was on her, his head beside hers. He withdrew slowly, leaving only the tip inside her then plunged forward again while penetrating her skin and drinking from her once again.

She screamed this time. "Yes! More, please, Imendand."

He acquiesced, pumping in and out of her slowly but steadily. It was maddening. She clutched at him, raking her nails down his back and shoulders. "Harder, please. Faster," she begged.

His pace picked up and the noises coming from his mouth were no longer words. He pounded her into the ground, his dick reaching places inside her no man had ever been. His firm but smooth head bumped her cervix with every thrust and she relished the tactile sensation. Lifting her head from the ground to reach him, she laid kisses along his collar bone. This must have pleased him, because he slid his forearm beneath her head, pressing her face against his chest.

"Bite. Drink. We will be one, my beautiful Sinnis."

She had human teeth, not fangs, and she didn't break the skin on the first try. She did on the second attempt, but not enough and so Imendand sliced a deep gash just above his heart with his nail and pressed her face against it again. The first taste hit her tongue in a burst of flavor. He was spicy and sweet, his blood thick and powerful. She lapped at it, enjoying the taste but then sealed her lips around the wound and sucked.

Imendand began to fuck her again in earnest as she pulled prana from his body. It had never been like this. Sex had never been this good. Having someone drink his blood had never been gratifying. Making his children was a duty, not pleasure. His relief at finding her, the warmth of her surrounding his member, his life flowing inside her was all too much. He knew nothing would ever be the same again. He emptied his seed into her and she groaned against him with every spurt.

Imendand, as if in a type of trance, spoke, "I, Imendand Belial Maru, give you my name freely and the power over me that comes with that knowledge. I can do none other than invoke your name, Christy of the Belial family line, binding you to my side for all time. In the beginning there were only males. Therefore, each will leave his father and mother and cleave to his Sinnis, and the two shall be made one flesh. So they depend on Ud and Ki no longer but will hunger only for each other. What has been joined together, none can put asunder."

Even as his much heavier form lay resting on top of her, Christy knew that something was happening. She could feel his blood inside her, moving throughout, changing her. She was sexually satiated but hungered for more. The necklace was heavy against the hollow of her neck and she felt it slip from his shoulders to lay resting over her clavicles. She felt the cold weight of it settle against her skin and then it grew warmer as it sank under the flesh.

She brought her hand up to feel it and she came against nothing but skin. Imendand's head had risen slightly and his breathing had slowed, but he stared at the place where the necklace had become a part of her, indeed looking very much like a birthmark. He still moved in and out of her slowly, each time bringing a shudder as if he wanted to stop but couldn't. Then warmth enveloped her, and the blackness took her like a comforting blanket.

ELEVEN

Nathalia had returned to the site of the tear in the veil after dawn to find the vrykolak unaffected by Ud's light. The pack had to be children of a Nephilim, not Akhkharu as she had originally thought. Their existence grated on her; she had forbidden the sharing of Nephilim blood with humans. Whoever had sired these had broken her law. She tried to let it go, but found it hard to relinquish her ingrained beliefs. Kiyahwe herself had admonished Nathalia for her prejudices. They were all Her children and had every right to life. Kiyahwe had said they all served a purpose, Her purpose. Vrykolak were not an abomination.

Eiran must have come to the same conclusion. He stood beside them. Nathalia joined him. These were keeping the Shinar from crossing through. They continued to hold the line. Nathalia knew without asking that no other life had been absorbed by the Shinar; their portal was no larger than it had been when she'd left. The mother and her children, who had watched the abusive head of their family die by the claw and fang of the vrykolak pack, were safely settled in the women's shelter on the Daughters' compound.

The werewolves parted, spreading to allow her room beside her Nephilim. She appeared human and her proximity to the glow emboldened the people gathered. If she could be so near maybe the monsters would let them pass unharmed, the masses thought. They took a step forward almost in unison. Nathalia knew what she had to do. Their secret could not be kept any longer. She told Eiran what she needed and he complied. The two of them disappeared and then materialized in their true forms.

The people gasped. Nathalia knew how impressive Eiran would look to those who had never seen a Nephilim. He was taller than any human and had giant wings. He practically glowed, though they couldn't see it as well as she. His arm, like hers, had been transformed into a short sword. They projected their armored images to the humans' minds though in reality they stood naked.

She spoke, but did not move her mouth, wanting to impress upon those in attendance her power. *You must leave this place.*

"They can't any more than I could."

Nathalia and Eiran spun around to face the origin of that voice. It was recognizable. This was the man who had been torn in half when he played the rope in a tug of war between the Shinar and Kiyahwe. Nathalia had watched it happen. His name was Will something. That had only been a short time ago, but Will was much changed. Just as Harith Samsiel had described, the Shinar must have replaced his lower half with one of their own making. He was half human, half Shinar, but not in the same way as the Nephilim. He held a dagger of Shinar bone in his hand. This was the one who had come through the veil into Genevieve's nursery and hurt Juliet.

Will stood between them and the portal. The only way that could be was if he had come from the other side of the veil. He looked very smug, confident in his ability to best them. Nathalia knew that he thought the dagger he held was bathed in the blood of an unclaimed Sinnis. He thought he'd completed the recipe for a DakuAhu. Nathalia might be able to catch him unawares if he thought he was more armed than he actually was. She would have no trouble besting him if he was overconfident that his weapon could kill her. Samsiel had actually done the right thing in allowing Will to hurt Juliet. He had won them a small battle. It might be enough.

"I am the chosen vessel for Those Who See and Observe. I speak for Those who will not be named. Step aside and let the small-minded creatures of this world come to Them and They, in Their infinite goodness, will allow you half-breeds to live. They only ask for what is theirs, the life of this planet, in exchange for Their absolution of the criminal Yahweh's crimes."

All we have to do is let them consume all the life on mother earth and they will forgive us and Her and allow us to continue here on the lifeless planet. Nathalia wondered if her sarcasm came through in her mental telepathy.

"It would not be lifeless for long. They harvested from here once before, you know? The prehistoric world was packed with life. Your Yahweh did not fight them then. She feasted with them, gorging herself on the prana of the dinosaurs. Those Who See and Observe made it possible for mammals to rise. When a world reaches maximum density, as this one has, They must step in to keep it from destroying itself. Humans will destroy this, ruining it for all life if the Shinar do not stop them. They are the balance."

"No," Eiran barked more than spoke. "The Shinar know that they are out of time. They do nothing for the good of earth. They are hungry spoiled children. They know the time of Sinnis is upon us. They know that the One is here. They know Ishtar reincarnate will protect this world from their gluttony if we can hold the veil until she is mature."

There was activity within the Shinar ranks. They were agitated by what Eiran had said. They could hear. Their chosen had lied to them. He had not killed the One. Will blanched. They told him that he would suffer for his treachery.

"You do not accept Their proposal then?"

Absolutely not. They have nothing to bargain with. Nathalia prepared for the attack she knew was coming. She tried to push her will into the man's mind, but found it impossible. The Shinar part was taking over the human. His mind was not completely his own. She didn't have her normal power of influence over him.

"You must be Nathalia. You were quite foolish to choose the affections of a half-breed over Their love. You should have fulfilled your destiny. They would have allowed you and your women to rule this world and whatever form of life sprang up in the absence of humans. Now you will die with the rest."

Will moved fast, maybe quicker than Nephilim were able. He sliced through the necks of three vrykolak before Nathalia could react. She had expected him to attack her first and was unprepared for the slaughter of what she now knew were noble beasts.

Will laughed and held his dagger up for them to see. "It gains power with every life it claims, but I guess you knew that, didn't you, Ereshkigal?" Calling her by her ancient name reminded her of the time when she had been hurt and killed by the half-breeds and their children. "How many threads have you cut? How many half-breeds have you ended, gathering their life within you? How strong would you become if you turned now and killed the one beside you?"

He gave her a moment to consider. Will thought he was planting the seed of doubt and allowing it time to grow. This was the moment Eiran had expected from their first meeting. She was supposed to kill the half-breeds for the Shinar, but she would not do what they wanted. Not when they told her and certainly not now. Nathalia used Will's time allowance to share her plan with Eiran silently. Will pleaded with her, his concern clearly fraudulent. "They showed me how grateful they can be. They made me immortal. They gave me a part of themselves. They offer you the world! If it does not sway you to think of what They could give you, think on what They could take from you. They taught me the dangers of displeasing them. It would be smart to stop interfering."

Will moved to end the life of yet another vrykolak, but this time Nathalia was ready. She punched him in the chest, and he flew back and hit the ground. The impact should have knocked the dagger out of his hand, but she could now see that he wasn't just holding it. It was fused in his grasp. The Shinar were taking no chances that it would be lost to them and recovered by one such as her.

Will jumped up. "You chose the wrong side. Again."

He lunged at her, but Nathalia evaded his clumsy attack. Will was a bully, not a warrior. She met his every thrust with a parry, feigning loss of power. Now that Will had brought her attention to it, she could feel the increased strength that the lives she had claimed gave her. The silver threads of almost a dozen Akhkharu had gathered in the birthright stone that lay in the hollow of her neck. Will was no match for her now.

Nathalia slowed down enough for Will to imagine he had an opening. It stung when the sharp edge of his dagger was dragged through her upper arm. It was not a mortal blow. Even with her allowing him to cut her, the arm, a mere flesh wound, was the best he could do. She dropped to the ground, allowing Will to stand over her, gloating. She screamed mentally, filling the nonverbal sound with anguish, and writhed as if in pain.

She tried to move on to the next step in her plan. She was supposed to act dead. Will had never seen a Nephilim die by the work of a DakuAhu. He wouldn't know what to expect. The problem was that Nathalia couldn't stop screaming. Something was horribly wrong. She wasn't faking the pain. It was excruciating.

Nathalia was actually dying.

She looked to the wound in her arm, still dripping with blood when it should have healed almost instantly. She could see her thread of life had been cut. Its ends flapped in the air, unsure of which way to go. The dagger Will brandished was a DakuAhu. It didn't matter that it was Juliet's blood and not Genevieve's. It was every bit as magnetic to the threads as the birthmark which made her into a walking DakuAhu.

Eiran knew every thought in her head, such was their bond. He attacked Will with none of the reserve Nathalia had shown. He put distance between his dying Sinnis and the DakuAhu, being careful not to be nicked by it. As they fought, Nathalia grabbed the ends of her severed lifeline and tried to tie them back together. Only she could see them, she knew. It didn't work. They floated out of the breach in her skin and down to the hollow of her neck, where the birthstone waited patiently for its prana offering. They connected with their goal and began to reel in the rest of life from her body.

She wished for her voice back for the minuscule amount of relief a cry would afford her from the unimaginable pain as the string tore from the places it was sewn throughout her body. As the silver thread of life unstitched itself, she came unseamed. She had seen what became of those who met their end on the tip of the DakuAhu, but she did not break down. Her body did not return to the elements from which it was made. There was no flash as flame ate the air. She did not become a pile of earth in a puddle of water.

Her skin sealed itself as the last of her thread gathered in her birthmark. She was lucky. She wasn't just immortal; she could not be killed by any means. Eiran's love, her place as his Sinnis, had given her something that even the Shinar could not give, something that they could not take from her.

Eiran had no such gift from her love. If the DakuAhu pierced his flesh, he would die. She could not allow that. He had forced Will to bring the DakuAhu away, allowing her to gather her own thread. It was a gamble and one she didn't intend to waste. Will thought she was dead and Eiran kept him with his back turned to where she lay. Very quickly, she cut through Will's spine. Just a swipe was all it took to sever the human part from the Shinar. Will had sustained many small injuries from Eiran, but her Nephilim was not the living breathing DakuAhu. She was.

Will's top half still fought, slashing at Eiran with the dagger. Nathalia severed the dagger clasping hand from his arm. Will screamed. He had tasted immortality and was more sensitive to its loss because of it. He wasn't Nephilim. He did not unravel and return to the elements. He just died, his top half hitting the ground like so much meat. Will's lifeline gathered in Nathalia's birthmark, but it barely registered. The euphoria of gathering the prana from his Shinar half was near paralyzing.

The Shinar weren't merely filled with life, they *were* life. She hadn't gathered even half of what the Shinar part had to offer and Nathalia already felt like an atomic bomb. Her birthmark, unable to contain the energy, began dispersing the prana to every cell in her body. Her molecules vibrated on a higher frequency than was natural.

As quickly as it started, it was over. Her body absorbed the power and adjusted to the new higher levels. She smiled at Eiran.

She could read the concern in his face and wanted to ease it. *I'm fine. Don't worry. Where is the DakuAhu?*

She waited for his reply but all she got was silence. He closed his eyes. *What's wrong? Are you ill? Were you hit?* Eiran opened his eyes. Very slowly.

A blink was all it was. Nathalia looked around. The people who stood on the edge of the clearing were eerily still, waiting for their chance to die. The vrykolak, unmoving, guarded the line. Eiran was a statue. It was like the whole world was frozen in time, except for her. She turned to the tear in the veil. The Shinar were there, staring out at her, their rage barely contained. They had lost another portion of their power to this world. She could feel the part of them inside her pulling at everything around her.

This wasn't right. This power wasn't for her. She couldn't contain it. She concentrated on time and imagined a bubble around her. She slowed down the tempo inside her bubble to match the world. She dripped sweat from the effort, but was rewarded with Eiran's arms wrapping around her. Not wanting to hurt him, she moved slowly, sensing that she was still not yet on the correct frequency. She laid her head on his shoulder.

When she reached equilibrium, she tried to pop her virtual bubble. Nothing happened. The space inside, around her and Eiran, continued to slow down. The world around sped up until they couldn't even tell what was happening. Events were blurred and people were streaks. There was a strobing effect of days and nights passing quicker than seconds.

There was nothing they could do. So they held onto each other and the small wisp of reality it afforded.

✑

THE FIRST thing Christy noticed upon waking was the absence of discomfort of any kind. At the very least she should have been sore from sleeping for so long. She didn't know how long, but from how she felt, like she might never need to sleep again, she knew she'd gotten plenty of rest.

The next thing she noticed was that she was in a real bed. A really nice bed with high-quality sheets. The familiar weight of a male's arm fell across her side, recognizable even though it had been ages since she'd felt it. She snuggled back into the owner of that arm. His cock, which lay between her legs as if he'd been inside her when they fell asleep, hardened.

"You are awake."

The fat mushroom head of his dick had now grown until it protruded from between her legs, like some overdeveloped clitoris. "So are you." She gathered the pre-cum from its slit with her finger and spread it. It jumped and Imendand moaned.

Imendand.

She suddenly remembered everything. Being tied and left waiting. The joy of finally being acknowledged as his Sinnis. The long-awaited delight of being fucked properly. The spice of his blood. After that was blank. Well, not exactly blank. She had a vivid memory of intense pleasure. She didn't remember everything; she had no idea how they had gotten into bed or even where the bed was.

"Where are we?"

"My home. Our home," he corrected himself. "It lies along a tributary of the Nile. We are safe here. No one can find this place."

"I can't remember coming. How did we get here?"

Imendand moved slowly, pushing his penis back and forth between her clenched thighs in a mime sexual motion. Each time it showed, pushing out in front, Christy swirled her fingers over the impressive smoothness. "I remember you coming several times," he teased. "I tabalu'd us home for your conversion. I wanted you to be comfortable and I didn't know how long you would be unconscious. I am glad I did since now we are waking together in bed. Having you here makes me want you so badly."

Christy arched her back, angling so that he could penetrate with the next slow thrust. "I may have some blank spots in my memory, but I don't recall you being the type to ask."

He gripped her hip, clamping her to the bed as he entered her achingly slow. "I wasn't asking. I was warning." He slid his other arm under her neck and, bending his elbow, palmed her opposite shoulder. Flexing his muscles tightened them around her neck and her hands flew up to his forearm.

He pulled out and speared her again. "This will be short, but I will enjoy it very much." He picked up the pace but this position, while relaxing, did not give him the penetrating depth he craved. He turned them so she was facedown on the bed and he could pile drive her down into the mattress.

It was silent save the sound of their flesh slapping together. His grunts were added, and it was music to Christy's ears. His pleasure was hers. He was using her, enjoying her, and she had no doubt it was on a grander scale than she had ever been enjoyed before. This position was amazing. With every forward move his length rubbed that spot inside her that she'd never known was there. The pressure built until it was almost pain and she screamed into the pillow. Her muscle spasms clenched so tightly that she feared she might pinch him off. Her toes curled as she tried to stay still for him. When her limbs twitched with every thrust, her body spent from her sudden climax, he slowed and then stopped, still buried.

He put his weight on her, making the panting she had been doing impossible. He moved her hair to the side and she turned her face so that he could see her profile. He nibbled her ear and then said, "Your pussy feels incredible, but maybe I'd like to sample another of your pleasure-giving places."

He put one giant sausage finger between her lips. She sucked it obediently. When it was thoroughly moistened, he gave her a second finger to lubricate. Still inside her, careful not to pull out of her pussy, he reached between their bodies. Sliding the fingers wet from her mouth between her butt cheeks until he found her tight asshole, he toyed with it, circling, until at last she lifted slightly, pushing against his hand. "So eager." She could hear the smile in his voice, but she didn't mind. He pushed one finger in to the first and then second knuckle. "I can imagine how it would feel to be in you here, you moaning, writhing beneath me, not sure if you wanted me to keep going or stop. But that is not for today. You are so tight around just my finger. I think it will take some work and practice to fit my member."

He lifted his ass, pulling out of her. The bed dipped when he lifted his weight off her, his hands on the mattress. "Turn over," he commanded. Disappointed that she was not going to get the ass fucking she so longed for, she obeyed, thinking he would just finish in her pussy missionary style. He didn't. He sat back on his heels, his butt barely touching her pelvis, and stared at her. "So beautiful." He leisurely stroked his length with one hand and palmed her breasts with the other. He had studied her while she slept, recovering from her conversion, but he knew she'd not gotten a good look at him, so he gave her time now.

Christy realized at once that this was not Belial. Imendand was not the man she'd been thinking was her Nephilim. Imendand had claimed her when Belial had abandoned her. Looking at him now, she wondered if she had ever really been fooled. While they did look similar, they were clearly not the same person. Where Belial had been golden, Imendand was copper. His head was bald, and they had the same Egyptian look, but Imendand was larger and had body hair in all the normal places most men did. She rejoiced at the feel of it against her palms as she gripped his thighs. He allowed her to take over stroking his member when her hands replaced his.

He tucked another pillow under her head, propping it up. "Hands above your head." She threw her arms up so they dangled over the pillows. Inching forward on his knees until they were chin level, he squeezed so that her biceps were tight against her ears, trapping her head. "Open your mouth."

No three words had ever turned her on more. She knew they weren't the three words most girls longed to hear, but they did more for her than those other three ever hoped to. The head of his dick was smooth and so filled with blood that it was practically purple. He rubbed it like lipstick around the circle her open mouth made. She reached her tongue out and tasted his delicious cock. She was not disappointed.

"Later we will have lessons on how best to please me, but right now, I just need to feel the warmth of your mouth around me." He pushed into her mouth and pumped in and out of her face, each time getting further. She tried not to choke when he pressed against the back of her throat. She tried to use some techniques she had learned over the years, but he was so big that her mouth was just filled with him and her tongue could barely move. She managed to relax her throat when he pushed hard enough to force the tip past her tonsils. She didn't get to taste his cum, so deep down her throat was he when he came. He clenched her hair as his cock jumped, spurting his seed practically directly into her stomach.

Spent, he collapsed beside her. Christy lay there, feeling satisfied, and then sat up. She put her hand to her face and groaned inwardly. Her face was as naked as the rest of her. She had been so caught up in the morning's activities that she hadn't thought about what a mess she must look. She hadn't had the energy to put on makeup in goddess knows how long. The last time she had even thought about her war paint had been before she'd fixed the tear in Genevieve's nursery. She buried her face in her hands.

Imendand slid off the bed to kneel in front of her. She turned her face away. He put his hand on her knee. "Did I hurt you?" His question was whispered; he feared he had gone too far. She shook her head no, but he knew something was wrong. "I never want to hurt you. I would never strike you or do anything out of anger. I push the boundaries only for our sexual gratification."

"It's not that. I…I'm embarrassed."

"There is no reason to be ashamed. What we derive pleasure from is our own business. No one can judge us."

He wasn't addressing the issue she was having, but his words struck a chord with her. Imendand would never lash out at her, hurt her, or make her feel ashamed of what she desired. She could only imagine what freedom of fear could do for her. She had never been without it. "I need my makeup."

Imendand didn't say anything. He stood and took her hands in his, pulling them first away from her face and then used them to pull her to her feet. He led her to what she assumed was the bathroom, though it was so much larger than any she'd ever seen that it looked more like a bathhouse. The tub was large enough to do laps in and was filled with water from a continual flow in the wall beside it. Above was a relief carving depicting life along the Nile and the water came from the representation of the river. There were steps into the pool on either side. Imendand took her to a mirror in the far wall.

Christy was amazed by her reflection. Her hair, which should be bedraggled, lay perfectly over her shoulders and down her back. Her skin was smooth and nearly poreless, cheeks rosy, lips pink, and eyes highlighted by lush lashes. The shading on her lids was more perfect that she'd ever managed with any product. Then she understood. "When you reformed me, you perfected me. You took all my blemishes away."

"I did nothing to your appearance. You are as you always were. My blood flows in you now. You see yourself as I see you, through my eyes. You are so beautiful, so perfect, I did not need to alter a thing. I made your eyes as close to your original piercing sky blue, but they have changed somewhat. It is not because I desired a change, but our eyes are different than that of humans'. I would have your eyes the same, but I could only give them a bit more blue flecks than would be normal, not return them to your natural color. The conversion demands certain modifications."

It was all a little much for Christy. Imendand thought she was perfect. He hadn't wanted to change her in any way. No one had ever felt that way about her, and certainly no one had ever felt compelled to say such things to her. "Come on, Romeo, I need a bath." She pulled him away and was glad he quit complimenting her before the point when he told her she was like the sun, more beautiful than the moon.

TWELVE

Any insecurity she might have felt for Imendand dissipated as he reformed their bodies. It seemed to take ages as he pieced them together cell by cell, but she could sense the world around them had slowed to a stop, waiting. In a flash they stood, face to face, and with his warm chiseled body pressed against hers, Christy knew they were perfectly suited for each other.

Unlike with Belial, Christy had no doubts with Imendand. There were no feelings of unworthiness, no frustrations, no nagging thoughts that he wasn't sharing everything. Now Christy knew the value of being able to survive tabalu with a Nephilim. When she was traveling with him through the earth like that, she could feel him inside her. Her very soul, if there was such a thing, was permeated with his. Their bodies were as one.

"Is it always like that?" she whispered.

She clung to him, savoring the sensations. She rested her head on his chest while the knee knocking pleasure subsided, completely unconcerned by their nakedness. Being moved in that way by Imendand was more intimate than sex, which, until experiencing it with him, she had never thought of as a very intimate act anyway. Now that she'd had sex with him a number of times, she wasn't sure if what she'd been doing with men prior qualified as the same act.

"No, never before have I felt so…"

"…connected." Christy finished his thought for him. She slid her arms from their place around his neck to rest on his chest. Placing her ear on top of his heart, she used its beat to steady her own.

Imendand was happy to give her time to enjoy the experience because he needed a moment too. Tabalu was how Nephilim moved themselves from place to place instantly. It was handy in battle, but it was a lonely way to travel. He had forgone the process almost entirely for ages because of how inhuman it made him feel. The world was much more crowded with humans now than in his time and they made him acutely aware that he had no one, especially since his brother had forgone any association with him thousands of years ago.

"Come. My brother has waited long enough. And then we must see to the tear. My pack can only hold humans back for so long."

Imendand stepped away from her and only then did Christy open her eyes and take in her surroundings. They were on a rock cliff, high above where most humans would come. The tree line was some feet below and through the cloud bank Christy could see the winding body of the Blue Nile. There was no one for miles.

Once the thought crossed her mind, she focused on it. She was aware of every living thing around them. The goat above them was coaxing her young to climb. There were few birds this high, but there were some here and there, nesting on the ground. Just below the surface was teaming with insects. This area was not void of life. It was just void of human life.

"You are hungry." Imendand said it as a statement. He could recognize the look in her eye and the way her mind searched for prana sources around them. He held his arm out to her. This was a utilitarian feeding, not a sensual one. They had things to do, and he did not want to get caught up.

"So soon? You said that your sex and blood, the life they contain, would feed me and I would think I've had enough of both for a while."

The rumble in Imendand's chest when he spoke was evidence of his own hunger. "You and I will never have enough of each other."

Knowing they had things to do, Christy tried to get her own mind off sex and how the sound of his voice made her want it even more. She took his outstretched hand in her own and lowered their now clasped appendage. She would not drink from him now. Not like this. She would not have him feel that providing for her was a chore. It would be done when they had time for pleasure. "That's not what I meant. I just…ate. How are we supposed to get anything done if I am hungry every five minutes?"

"We aren't supposed to get anything done. No one expects us to function properly for a while, until we have reached equilibrium, but we do not have such luxuries. We are needed. You need training in all aspects of being as I am. Hunger is at the very core of our nature. It is a beast that can overtake our humanity if we do not feed it. Tabalu is not only how we travel; it is how we reconnect with the great mother Kiyahwe. When we travel through her, she undoes any nourishment we may have taken in prior. That is her Shinar nature and even with the dampening effect the earth has she cannot help but absorb some life from us as we pass."

He paused and tucked a stray strand of her blonde locks behind her ear. He was puzzled by his own actions. Being with Christy made him want to share everything with her. He wasn't sure he had spoken this much in the last decade put together. "I should have flown us here since it is a small distance, but I wanted to feel it again. I admit, it was done as a purely selfish act, but now I see it served another purpose. I needed to move you again in the Nephilim way, soon after the tabalu that changed you. It serves to bind us more closely until we are inseparable. I can feel it. More of you is in me and me in you with every pass through the great mother."

She stared at him, noticing for the first time how he glowed. Everything living around her glowed in its own way, the strength a measure of its prana. Imendand was like the sun when compared to the candle luminescence of other living things. She knew that even a human's blood, as filled with life as they were, would be nothing to her Nephilim's. She looked down at her own hand and could see Imendand's life flowing through her. She wondered if other Sinnis and Nephilim could see it and if she would sense it in others.

"Your brother is near?"

He gestured with his chin to a small cave opening just a little way further up the stone path naturally cut from the mountainside. "But I can't feel him. Not at all." She could not sense him as a source of prana, but more than that, she did not feel the pull Belial seemed to exert continually. It was the thing he had needed her for, to cut off that magnetic attraction he had from the world that threatened his peace every waking moment. Christy cocked her head to the side quizzically. She couldn't feel any higher forms of life.

"I have him shielded." Imendand pulled her along the path that narrowed as it reached the cave's entrance, pushing his arm behind him, forcing them into single file, unwilling to relinquish her touch.

She watched his back as they walked, her attention drawn to the ripple of muscles that each step drew. Until that moment she hadn't realized how sexy a male's back could be. The flexing of his perfectly formed butt was almost more than she could resist. She wasn't sure if it was their bond or the hunger feeding her attraction, but all she could think of was sinking her nails and teeth into the flesh of his rock-hard ass.

Imendand took them deep into the cave. It took less time than she expected for her eyes to adjust to the lack of light. She thought that here her hunger aided her, instead of hindering her ability to think clearly. The cave was filled with life; illuminating prana shone in every nook and cranny. As they went further, the walls made an abrupt change from scraggly and crumbled to hard and smoothed.

The narrow cave opened into a great cavern, but this room was not naturally occurring. Christy could tell that at first glance. The floor was much too level and the walls were elaborately carved.

Imendand explained, "Our mother could not be placed in the mother's tomb. Her presence would present a danger to them all. I made her own sacred burial site."

Christy released his hand in order to more closely examine the nearest carving. It was more detailed than anything she'd seen and done in such a masterful way that the figures pictured seemed to breathe, their clothes moving in the imaginary breeze. "You did this? All of them?"

He dipped his chin once, a slow nod, uncomfortable with how anxious he was. Her opinion mattered far more than he remembered anyone else's ever mattering. He had decorated this place for a dead woman, thinking no one would ever see it beyond himself and possibly his brother. He found himself wishing he could have done more.

"It's beautiful, Imendand." She reached out to touch it but stopped herself mere millimeters above the carvings. Maybe they were actually alive, like the growths in the caves of Sonora her mother had taken her to see as a child, and the oils in her skin would destroy them. She didn't want to risk it. She had actually cried some years later when she heard that someone had broken the butterfly formation at Sonora Caverns. It had been the only formation of its kind in the known world but even in its rarity, it could not touch the value of Imendand's creation. "Amazing. It must have taken you forever to do this all on your own."

"It did. Many hundreds of years were spent. If not perfect when I finished, I would rub the stone smooth and start again. When I emerged, the world had changed around me. I did not recognize it, nor my brother, once I had found him."

The mention of Belial brought Christy's attention back to the task at hand. They were here to deal with him. She looked around until she spotted Belial. He was huddled on the ground, near a large sarcophagus, his wings stretched out behind him.

"He was always so vain. That much never changed. When I set this trap, I left enough earth within my shield that he could shift his size, hiding his wings if he so chose. I knew he would come in all his glory, his unaltered form. Even though it causes him discomfort, forces him to kneel to allow them space, his vanity will not allow him to hide his wings."

Belial's head snapped up and Imendand tucked Christy safely behind him but not before she saw the hatred in the trapped Nephilim's eyes. He clearly blamed her for his predicament. It wasn't my fault, Christy thought. "Why did he need to find Gazbiyya so badly, anyway?"

"He swore to destroy her body eons ago. That is why I brought her here. I thought I would remain here with her forever. I knew no other way to shield her presence from him than to form my thickest and most secure shield around us. I split my time between carving and perfecting my ability. It was during this time that Kiyahwe spoke to me directly. She taught me of her history and helped me grow in skill. I can set a shield and leave it intact. I can even create a moving permanent shield as light as a second skin around those who carry my blood."

Now that he spoke of it, Christy could feel the shimmering invisible chain mail surrounding her. She had his blood inside her but from the way he spoke she knew, "I'm not the only one who carries your blood." She shook her head in confusion. "But Nathalia said that there was only one Sinnis for every Nephilim. I thought I was special…"

Imendand took her face in both his hands and forced her to look at him. "You are. For me there is only you. You are my Sinnis, Christy. Only you can tabalu with me. I have fed my blood to humans before, but they are my children, not my mate."

"How many?" Her question was little more than a whisper, but it wasn't shyness that made her speak softly. It was anger. The thought of anyone else tasting his blood enraged her. It was for her alone.

"Over the ages there have been hundreds, maybe more. Currently I have a vrykolak pack numbering two and ten. I choose for my own the worst amongst human ranks, those with the darkest hearts, the blackest thoughts."

"And to *those* you give the gift of eternal life?!" Christy knew vrykolak meant werewolf basically, because that was what Billy was. Their strength was unparalleled, surpassed only by that of the Nephilim.

"Theirs is a life of servitude. They die, more often than not, in the most horrific of ways. It is a sentence, a punishment, not a gift. As their maker I control every part of their lives. I don't allow them to shift between forms. They are reduced to little more than beasts, always hungry and rarely allowed to eat, with no real choices. They are forbidden, unable to hurt the ones they want the most." He stepped away from her then and approached Belial. "That is what I will do for you, brother. You will taste my blood. You will wear my shield. It will serve as your chain. You will not kill. You will not feed. You will not touch nor destroy Mother's body."

"No!" Christy yelled, bringing Imendand's attention back to her. "Your blood will make him a monster. That's what Nathalia has been warning us all about. A Nephilim must never drink the blood or taste the flesh of another Nephilim. It is the first of your laws."

"He is already a monster, just a beautiful one. He will be an Akhkharu, but one incapable of killing. It is the only way I can protect him, protect the world from his pull. My blood will give him peace from his hunger and rest from his constant pursuers." Once again, Imendand extended his arm, but this time offering it to Belial instead of Christy.

Though it hadn't worked with Belial, she didn't hesitate to try it with Imendand. "I claim right of Sinnis. I alone provide you with the prana you require. My blood, my sex, will sustain you as yours will me." She acted with more bravado than she felt, pulling Imendand's arm away from Belial's reach and wrapping it around her back. Stretching on her tipiest of toes, she put her lips on Imendand's neck for the briefest of kisses.

Razor sharp incisors slid into her mouth at the proximity of his vein, filled with prana-rich blood so close to the surface. She salivated when she felt his heart rate quicken. "Your blood is mine and I won't share it." She scraped his skin with her teeth gently, carefully building the anticipation. This would be the first time she had ever bitten him with her new teeth, and she instinctively knew to savor it.

"Wait," Imendand commanded.

Christy almost rebelled right then at the thought that he might deny her or try to talk her out of it. In her peripheral vision she saw Belial's prison go solid black. Imendand was only trying to give them privacy and that told her it was every bit as intimate and important an act as she had thought. He wrapped his arms around her tightly and lifted her feet off the ground so that she could easily get a better angle at his neck.

"You have every right. I offer you freely what is yours." His voice was deeper than usual, thick with need.

Christy pushed her thoughts of Belial from her mind and how his rejection had stung. He had no place in their special moment. She focused on how different it felt in Imendand's arms. He had never, not once, denied that she was his Sinnis. He had never denied her what she needed. Imendand had never denied her. Period. And as her teeth slid into his flesh and his life force poured into her mouth, she knew he never would.

She had tasted his blood before, but this was different. His skin healed as soon as her teeth were clear of it and she was forced to bite him again. This time she didn't just let the blood flow over her tongue, she pulled from him. He groaned and her feet touched the ground again as his knees buckled. She wrapped her legs around his waist and when he sat back on his heels her butt was cradled in his lap, his erection hot against her.

Christy nibbled her way from his throat to his neck, stopping along the way for a suck whenever a spot tickled her fancy. It was decadent in a way she had never experienced. He was hers to use in any manner she desired.

He lifted her off his lap easily with one arm and used the other hand to position his cock at her aching entrance. She had made the claim, but it was now he who would collect. He pushed her down around his length as his own fangs sliced through her. They were joined in every way possible.

He took a few pulls only, just enough to count as a feeding. She nibbled her way along his jawline and then pressed her mouth against his. She knew he could taste himself on her lips and if it did to him anything close to what it did to her then they wouldn't stay. Surprisingly, he sat stoic and even pulled his hands from her body.

Christy eased back from her kiss to study his face. There was fire in his eyes, that he felt passion was undeniable. She did not understand why he didn't act until he spoke. "I am yours. Take what you need. Use my body and blood and be satisfied."

She knew then what he wanted. Clasping her hands behind his neck, she leaned back so that her torso did not touch his. She dug her heels into the ground behind him and lifted almost off him completely before pounding down again. Over and over she slammed down, always clenching him tightly on the upstroke. It was an angry frenzied coupling. There was little noise above the slapping of skin for several minutes.

She watched as he struggled to give her this moment of control, his palms itching to grab her, his hips aching to thrust at his tempo. When she stopped, neither of them had climaxed. He asked, "Satisfied?"

She did not trust her voice at first and only shook her head no, but at the look of dejection on his face she stammered, "It's not you, it's me." She laughed again and shook her head at the cliché. "I mean that I'm not good at…I don't like…I can't come when I'm on top. I'm not good at being in charge. I have to give up control, surrender. I need aggression and sometimes to feel helpless. Other girls think I'm crazy not to like girl on top and maybe I am. Maybe I'm defective. My head is just so screwed up…"

Imendand's hand clamped over her mouth, effectively shutting her up without warning. "I won't hear you belittle yourself, your desires. Not now, not ever." He leaned them so that her back rested on the ground and he hovered over her. Her eyes widened when she felt him grow impossibly large inside her. That look, over his hand, made a beautiful image. "Did it never occur to you that my tastes complimented yours?"

He pulled back and rammed into her and she cried out from behind his hand. His eyes went solid red, lid to lid, corner to corner. He slowly morphed back into that image of an Akhkharu that she had seen outside her shield those many nights ago. "That you need aggression because I need to be aggressive? That you are a sexual submissive because I am Dominant? That you want to feel helpless because I want to trap you, bind you, tie you, compress you, and fuck you until my heart is content?"

Christy's eyes rolled back in her head. His coarse words combined with his predatory looks were too much, too perfect. Imendand tightened his grip on her mouth and forced her head to the side. His words were little more than a growl in her ear when he commanded, "Put your feet high in the air. Use your hands to hold them there. Open wide to me. I am going to punish you for doubting that we are perfectly suited for each other in every way. Nod. That is what you want, isn't it?"

She obeyed. Nodding furiously beneath his mitt, she raised her feet to the sky and gripped her ankles. She could not see his face anymore, her face pushed to the side, but she heard his joy at her obedience.

"Be still while I take my pleasure in your body." He removed his hand from her face and, gripping her hips so tightly she knew they would bruise, he began to fuck her in earnest. She did her best to freeze in the position he had her. It allowed her to focus on the sensations of his cock filling her more fully, threatening to tear her apart, and she loved it. She thought of how much more capable he, as a Nephilim, was of dominating her completely than any other being in existence and it almost pushed her over the edge. She was quickly reaching the point of no return but she needed his permission to orgasm.

She tried to plead with him using her eyes but without turning her head. Her voice appropriately submissive, she begged him, "Please, Imendand. May I come? It feels so good, I'm afraid I won't be able to stop myself." Her voice jolted with every thrust.

"You may, but first tell me this is what you want, what you were born for. Say that there is nothing wrong with you, that you are perfect." He reached between them and circled her clit, forced from its hood by her spread legs. With the pad of his thumb, he stroked with a constant pressure as she struggled to make the words during the barrage of sensual delights, as if he could coax the words from her constricted throat. "Look at me when you say it, Christy."

When she made eye contact, desperate to do as he wanted, the words poured out. "I was born to please you. You give me exactly what I want. I want to be fucked like an animal in the dirt, knowing that you could kill me at any moment, nearly dying from pleasure every time you take control. I am… perfect because you want me."

The hand not bringing her to the brink of insanity with its perfectly pressured ministrations closed around her throat, pinning her to the ground. He wasn't choking her, but the reminder that he could was just enough. She came hard, bucking and screaming herself hoarse. He stopped his pumping, the involuntary clenching of her internal muscles enough to trigger his own orgasm. He roared as he filled her with his semen and collapsed on top of her, his weight like icing on the cake.

She released her ankles and wrapped her arms and legs around him. After a few minutes she said, "I can't really breathe, Imendand."

He pushed up and smiled at her, though in his current form, it looked threatening, like an animal showing its teeth. "Good thing you don't have to." He stood and helped Christy to her feet, her legs very unsteady.

"What? I don't breathe?"

"No. We breathe, but we don't need to."

"That should make deep throating a little easier," she quipped.

He grabbed a handful of her glorious locks and held her still for his kiss that silently told her she should be careful not to say such things when he was feeling so weak to resist her. He tried to ignore the ache in his balls at her casually mentioning the act he so longed for her to perform. They had time. They would make time for that sooner or later. He promised himself it would be sooner rather than later.

Imendand's hair began to recede and his appearance returning to that of Belial's brother. He snapped his fingers, and the shield went transparent again. Christy wasn't as comfortable with her nudity as most of the Daughters and wished she had some clothes.

Imendand didn't seem concerned with it and she had never known Belial to wear a stitch. She mentally shrugged. Oh well, she thought, it's not like either of them hasn't seen everything I've got already.

"He came here to destroy Mother's body."

"Why?"

"He cannot turn off his ability. Without a shield maker like you, willing to spend her life as his personal protector, he can have no rest. He thinks that by destroying Mother's body, he can cut his power off at the source. Even though now he knows that I will never allow that, he has other crimes to atone for."

"Like what?" Sure, he was an arrogant prick, but she hadn't known him to be a malicious criminal.

"He nearly wiped our mother's bloodline from the face of the earth while I was here training and honoring her. He killed all who showed only skill in attracting and used those who could repel or shield until they were old and incapable of reproducing. It is the sworn duty of every Nephilim to protect his mother's bloodline. He should have done his duty and waited for his Sinnis."

"Can he hear us in there?"

"Mostly."

"Why isn't he saying anything, defending himself?"

"He cannot. The shield is a vacuum. There is no air around him."

Christy stared at Imendand. He had just told her as a matter of fact that he'd been suffocating his brother for how many days now. He had said that they didn't need to breathe, but it couldn't have been comfortable.

"Do you dislike how he is being treated during his imprisonment?"

Christy watched Imendand's face. She wondered if this was a test of her submission. He was certainly more of an expert on his brother than she was. "Whatever you feel is best, is best."

"I only desire your submission during sex. In all other ways, in all other circumstances, you are my equal, my partner. I set this trap when I was alone. I planned to give him my blood, release him, shield him, and control him, but you claimed right of Sinnis. I did not begrudge you that dominance, did I?" he asked rhetorically. "Together we must devise a new plan. Would you like to hear what he has to say?"

"I don't really care what he has to say. He didn't care about what I wanted when I thought…never mind. I don't want him to be tortured any longer." The air rushed by Christy, moving her hair and sending a wave of sensations across her skin, as it filled the now available void of Belial's prison.

Belial took a deep breath. "You cared more for Mother's body than you ever did her bloodline. You would not allow me to destroy her dead body. You, brother, forced my hand. I killed them to save them. They were like me, alluring to everyone. Their gift could not discern between a good and noble person or a rapist. Their lives were ones of terror that only death could end."

"You should have protected them!" Christy had never heard Imendand yell, and she was glad his anger was not directed at her. She wondered if perhaps she had the power to attract and if so, maybe that was the reason she so often ended up with the biggest assholes.

Belial seemed unphased and yelled back, "I tried!" He shook his head. The small movement made gold dust shake from his wings. Now that the sphere was filled with air, he looked like an angel figurine trapped in of one of those cheap snow globes filled with gold glitter instead of white. "I only killed the ones like me, with the power to attract with no control. I couldn't protect them. I couldn't get close to them. My presence only attracted more unwanted attention. I had to kill them."

"You said that before. What of those not like you, those like me, who could attract and repel at will? Why did they have to die?" Imendand didn't sound mad anymore. There was sadness in his voice. He looked at Christy and then reached out and took her hand. "I was lucky. The great Kiyahwe took pity on me and made a new bloodline of shield makers, but you couldn't have known that would happen when you wiped out the original one."

"You don't understand. It didn't happen like that. It was an accident that they died. I tried to bring them together under one household. One powerful and influential family ruled without question while you were hiding. I was with them and they shielded me in return for my service. I ensured they stayed in control, but I was ignorant of human biology. I did not know that breeding members of the same family too closely would result in…problems with fertility and other deformities. I was trying to consolidate the bloodline."

"Why interfere? Why not just let nature take its course?"

Did he just want to hear Belial say it aloud? Christy wondered. Imendand had said several times that his brother was arrogant and vain. Belial had clearly thought that he could manipulate the bloodlines and bring about the birth of a Sinnis early. "He did it for you." Imendand turned to her when she spoke, his brow furrowed not in anger, but confusion. "He thought he could get you your Sinnis early by concentrating the blood."

Imendand turned back to his brother. "I cannot believe it was such a selfless act."

"Nor was it as malicious as you think," Belial said. "I was being selfish. I did not want to travel the world, watching over the ever-growing number of women who showed your ability, so I caused them to interbreed. They lived together along the Nile, protected, loved, and even worshiped by their subjects. The throne passed to sons, not even I could push the humans away from patriarchy, but I did make sure it followed the mother. By the time I realized what was happening I could not sway the family from their course. I had done my work too well. They thought themselves above all other humans. They thought their bloodline alone was worthy. They thought they alone were descended from gods, that they were gods." Belial stretched as tall and proud as his prison would allow. "I loved Ankhesenpaaten. That idiot child husband loved her too. He thought he could father the next king and did not allow other men to couple with her. He ignored evidence to the contrary. Dead babies began to pile up, horrifying mutated children born of brother and sister, and still he would not allow her to lie with other men. He forced her to give birth to monster after dead lifeless monster." A tear, the first evidence of any true emotion besides anger that Christy had ever seen from him, rolled down his beautiful face. "I could not bear to see her pain. I killed him. I thought another man, not of her family, would step up and take her as his wife and become king. That is how it should have worked. The crown would sit on the head of the man she chose to marry." He wiped away the tear almost angrily and shook his head. "She would take no other. She loved her brother, the dead king. She died heartbroken and took away my shielding. I ran. I am exhausted from running. Over the centuries I have found a few, here and there, like you, Christy. Like with you, what I had to do to keep them loyal and devoted to me and my protection, made them forgo all other men."

"It's true. He tried to get me to sleep with Billy, but I couldn't bear it. I only wanted him." She turned to Imendand. "Except when I saw you it was like the spell was momentarily broken. I thought I was his Sinnis, but I knew from the second that I laid eyes on you that something was horribly wrong with him, something wrong with us being together." She paced, chewing on her thumbnail, which she noticed was much harder and perfectly shaped than ever before. She looked down at it and realized that she could feel through it. Her actual nails had nerves and she could feel them. She shook her head, trying to clear her mind of the distracting thought and the sensation of her hair on her shoulders threatened to tear her from reality. "I need to think. There is a solution to our problem here; I just need time to figure it out."

She sat on the only thing that marred the perfectly flat floor of the tomb besides the sarcophagus. The large stone was well worn from the ages Imendand had spent sitting on it, like a beloved couch in front of a TV in some sports lover's basement. *Could I take them both as lovers?* she wondered. She knew Camilla had successfully taken two men as mates, but their relationship was an anomaly in both the human and Nephilim world. Izzy was something special and he was not a Nephilim. Christy looked at the two brothers as they glared at each other. No, there was too much bad blood between them. Blood.

"I can shield him," she announced.

Imendand shook his head. "No. For that to work he would have to be in your presence always and I will not allow that. You are mine and I will not share you."

Well, that cleared up her previous line of thought. "I don't mean in the way I've been doing it. You said that you could make a movable shield for your vrykolak. That was your plan for Belial. He would drink your blood, take in your prana, and you would protect and control him. Can you teach me to make the second skin-like shield?"

"Yes, but it would do no good. You have claimed right of Sinnis. That, Christy, is a sacred oath. From now until the end of time, only you will feed from my blood and sex and I demand no less from you. Only I will savor your prana. I will not allow my brother to taste you. I will not allow you to break your vows to me."

"I just made those vows. I wouldn't…He already tasted…" The look in Imendand's eyes made her stop. They went from loving to enraged in a snap.

He turned his blood red orbs from her face and screamed at his brother, "You drank the blood of my Sinnis!"

"No, never," Belial managed before Imendand cut off his air supply again.

"He never took my blood, Imendand. Only you have that." Christy paused. She didn't know how to tell him what he needed to know. She didn't want to say it out loud.

She didn't have to. Imendand understood. If his brother had Christy's prana inside him but hadn't taken her blood, Imendand knew. "You had sex with my Sinnis!"

Imendand's rage went from emotion to a tangible thing. There was only his rage. His smooth and peaceful facade was gone in a flash, replaced by his hunger beast. He looked more giant silver-back gorilla than man. His claws gouged deep trenches in the floor he had spent decades smoothing. His anger was like standing in the world's strongest waterfall. Resistance was futile. Every thought was washed out of his mind except getting revenge. He couldn't hear anything but the roar of his fury. "The next thing you taste will be a small portion of the pain you have caused me."

Christy felt the rush of wind like before, but it didn't stop. She held her hair back so she could watch as Imendand pressurized the sphere with Belial inside. His beautiful, delicate wings were the first to go. They cracked and crumbled, soon followed by his body. Belial couldn't even scream in pain. The pressure was so great that his chest was crushed. He began to glow but not in the way that all life glowed. He was like a piece of burning coal.

"You have broken our laws, abandoned your duty, and betrayed me for the last time, brother. The DakuAhu will live up to its name. The Kill-Brother will taste your flesh and take your life."

Beside her Imendand laughed. It was a cruel sound and Christy knew it was up to her to defuse this bomb, otherwise Belial had no hope of surviving. She put her hand on Imendand's shoulder. He was standing beside her on all fours, reminding her of King Kong. "He didn't, Imendand. He never had sex with me. He only fed from me, from my orgasm."

"You think that makes it better?" he demanded. "I will destroy you for your betrayal, brother. Immense heat and pressure greater than that which the mother can produce in her depths will harden you. Immobile, you will adorn this chamber for eternity."

IMENDAND FLEW them home on tattered wings. He was the monster she'd seen those weeks ago on the other side of the Daughters' shield. Christy petted and cooed him all the way. She knew that only she was capable of bringing him back from the brink. She didn't know what was over that edge, but she knew she didn't want to see.

As they flew closer, Christy had her first view of the outside of the house. Imendand's home was a beautiful example of Mesopotamian architecture, but, she knew, it had all the amenities of a modern house. The natural setting, uncultured grounds, and native flora made it look like an ancient site. Perhaps it was. "How long has this been your home?"

"Since it was erected in my honor."

He hadn't really answered her question, but it gave her something. "And all that time you lived here with your vrykolak pack and human servants. It sounds like a life of luxury compared to the way Belial had to live." The sun on her skin felt better than it had the right to. She flopped onto her back on the ground to bask in its warm glory and found that the earth too provided her with warmth and comfort.

"Sympathy does not change the fact that he fed from you and in order to do that he had to give you pleasure that only I should provide." Imendand joined her, spreading his wings out so that they might absorb the strength of Ud's light.

"Honestly, did you expect me to stay untouched? I didn't even know I was anything special. I was just a girl trying to find joy in this world. I went through my share of boyfriends and of all of them, Belial treated me the... most gently." She turned on her side and propped herself up on her elbow, facing Imendand. "As far as 'giving me pleasure,' he didn't, not really. It wasn't pleasure. It was torture."

He didn't look at her. His forearm was thrown over his eyes as he reclined. "You are telling me that orgasms he gave you with his mouth were not pleasurable." He sounded disbelieving.

"He was feeding. It had nothing to do with me and what I wanted. I thought I was his Sinnis but he wouldn't touch me other than to feed. It meant nothing to me. It was...nothing compared to the pleasure you give me. If anything, it gave me perspective. It showed me that anyone with skill can play my body but nothing compares to the joy being with you, my Nephilim, brings."

Imendand turned to her then. He scooted forward until the lengths of their bodies were touching. He nuzzled her neck and whispered, "You are very smart." He ran his hand along her ribcage to her waist and over the swell of her hip. "That was the perfect thing to say. Did you practice it?"

She bent her knee and slid her calf along the back of his thigh. "In my head on the way here. I needed to calm you down so you would listen to my idea."

"Touching me like that, opening up so that it would be so easy to push inside you, is doing nothing to calm me down." She started to move away from him, but he stopped her. "Stay right where you are. It feels good to be so close. I'm not ready to give that up. Go ahead. I'll listen to your plan."

Being this close felt more than good. It was intoxicating. Not like with Belial. With him it felt like she was being forced, coerced. With Imendand, it felt like the best high she'd ever felt, one that she never wanted to end. She laid her head down and closed her eyes, shutting down the sensations she could so that she could concentrate on his touch. She hoped she could talk without slurring her words.

"What Belial has done is done. We can take advantage of it if he hasn't tabalu'd since his last feeding."

"He hasn't," Imendand ground out between clenched teeth. Seeing her prana glowing from within his brother had been what had pushed him to such extremes.

"If you can teach me how, I can shield him the way you do your vrykolak. He can serve me. I can send him away to protect the One and all the Daughters while they wait for their Nephilim. Don't you see? He can redeem himself for all the women of your bloodline that he killed or allowed to die. He has suffered enough, now he needs to make reparation for his sins."

Imendand hooked his arm under the knee resting on his hip and rolled them so that he was on top of her. He slowly pushed inside of her, watching her face as his chest hair scraped her hard nipples and his fleshy sword stretched her tight, wet sheath. He applied steady pressure, not stopping until he was seated to the hilt. "He will stay as and where he is until I can teach you. I must repair the veil. First, though, I will claim every part of your body as my own, imprinting my name on the very fabric of your being until you cannot even remember the world outside my body."

THIRTEEN

As a Sinnis Christy's power source was new, but her ability was unchanged and her talent was unparalleled. She just had to learn how to harness that power and the individual abilities came easily. In a matter of hours, she had erected a new shield for the Daughters, one which she did not need to reside inside of to retain.

They could have tabalu'd but Christy had fed until she thought she would burst. Imendand wanted her strength up for this, or that was what he told her. She knew he enjoyed their feeding sessions even more than she and she suspected his reasoning for their extended romp was more selfish than he let on. Nevertheless, she was more than happy to follow his lead. So they flew.

And what a flight it was.

Christy laughed at the thought that she was probably the only member of the mile-high club who'd had sex when both the pilot and the plane were the same thing.

The wind was almost deafening, but she could hear his voice as clear as a bell. "I fear you are not taking this as seriously as it should be."

Christy loved when he talked to her like that. He sounded so serious, like he wanted to chastise her, but found he could only spoil her. She tightened her legs around his waist, pressing her labia, stretched around the base of his cock, against his pubic bone. "I am taking it seriously, but it's impossible to get any leverage up here."

Imendand abandoned his ass play temporarily. He did so reluctantly. She was so responsive when he paid even the slightest attention to that other hole. Most women got so hung up on it that they couldn't enjoy. She came the hardest when he had a digit buried at least two knuckles deep in the back and his cock in the front. He had a surprise for her concerning that particular act, but it would have to wait. "Allow me."

Imendand did what he did best. He took control. Gripping her hips, again and again he penetrated. With his thumbs he angled her pelvis so that he slid along that slightly rough patch inside her that he knew drove her crazy. The tempo was quick, faster than any human could set, and it was just right for bringing on both of their orgasms.

She bit into his shoulder right before her release. She knew it was what he wanted. Her teeth had to breach the shield, her shield that he wore, before they cut the skin. It tasted like electricity, making her teeth itch. He came as soon as his blood hit her tongue. That was the exact moment when his blood tasted most alive, as if she could experience his orgasm as well as her own when the circuit was closed that way. His essence pumped into her mouth with the steady beat of his heart, and into her pussy with the irregular rhythm that his tightened balls set.

She let go of the clamp she had on his neck. She let gravity do its work and collapsed against his chest, struggling to catch her breath. She looked around, realizing they were resting on the ground. She hadn't felt the landing.

He sensed what she was thinking. "We fell."

"Flying and screwing might be even more dangerous than texting and driving. We're lucky the traffic is so light at 20,000 feet." Christy kissed his chest and lifted her head to smile at Imendand. She stood and smoothed out her skirt. He had pushed it up to the waist for the in-flight entertainment. "Where are we?"

Imendand pulled his jeans up from where they rested on his hips and zipped the fly. "The tear in the veil lies beyond those tree-covered hills."

"We don't have to walk, do we? I mean, I like being barefoot as much as the next girl, but this is the hill country and that would be one rocky stroll," she said, holding up her foot as if to show him how delicate it was.

He grabbed it and lifted, tipping her over. She would have fallen on her behind if not for the quick movement of his wing. She shrieked at losing her balance and then giggled. The kisses Imendand laid on the bottom of her foot tickled and the prehensile tip of his wing was doing wicked things to the back of her knee. Saying nothing, Imendand flipped her around onto his back and took to the skies again.

Christy gripped his shoulders, but not too tightly. She knew he'd never let her fall and hurt herself. She put her head next to his and watched the ground pass below them. Laying a kiss on his neck right below his ear drew a smile from him.

They circled, taking in the scene before landing. The tear was the largest Imendand had seen since Ishtar had walked the earth. It had allowed the Shinar to come through then and it was nearly that size now. That could not be allowed. Ishtar had battled the Shinar herself and barely won. She had been near all powerful then. From what Imendand had heard, the One, Ishtar reincarnate, was a mere child currently. As a human child, Genevieve would not stand a chance against the Shinar armies should they come through.

"What's wrong?"

Christy's small voice jolted him out of his thoughts. His worry must have shown on his face. "The tear is much larger than I expected."

"But you can close it, right? I mean, it's not the biggest you've ever seen, surely."

"There was one larger. Sealing it almost killed me. I had to use so great a length of lifeline that I hesitate to do so again."

"I thought that your lifelines were eternal."

"I feared for a long time that mine had been shortened to the point that I might actually age and die like my human half."

"Then you absolutely can't try it again." He raised his eyebrow and looked over his shoulder at her. "Your prana, your life, is mine, remember?" she explained. "I think I'm supposed to be able to seal it, somehow. Take us down. It'll come to me."

Encircling the tear stood a ring of Nephilim and their proximity seemed to enrage the Shinar. Nathalia, the First, also known as Ereshkigal, and her Nephilim stood behind them. They appeared frozen in their embrace. A bit further out, just inside the sphere of the Shinar's influence, stood Imendand's pack. They looked ragged but had remained firm. They had followed Imendand's instructions and not a single grain of prana had been collected by the Shinar since his vrykolak's arrival. If only Imendand had sent them sooner. He hadn't been thinking clearly then. All he could see, hear, or feel was his need to be near Christy.

Imendand set down in front of the alpha of his pack and communicated gratitude and praise for the werewolf's work. Christy doubted the monster heard a word of it. The vrykolak snarled at her, showing its blood-stained teeth and sounding its growl. It was more fox than wolf in color and its red eyes glowed with hatred. It was going to attack her. Imendand had warned her this might happen, and she knew what to do. Knowing and doing were two different things. Her fear overcame her, and she turned her back. It was a very reasonable response but the exact thing Imendand had said she must not do.

It pounced and Christy was shoved onto the ground face down. She looked to Imendand but he had stepped back, knowing his interference was not only unnecessary but could be detrimental. As Imendand's mate, she ranked above the alpha, but the beast was challenging her position. It could not draw her blood; that was against the rules. It could hurt her, and it was doing just that. The full weight of the vrykolak was on her back, crushing her ribs, straining her spine. It growled in her ear and snapped its deadly jaws at her face.

The growl changed, sounding more like the laugh of a hyena, and Christy felt a hard length growing between them. The werewolf couldn't kill her. It could exercise dominance over her in another way. Something inside her snapped. She wanted to be dominated, but only by Imendand. She wouldn't be raped. Never again.

She pulled energy from the sunlight and power through the body of Imendand's mother, the mother of her whole family line, and she super charged her shield. She didn't know what it felt like to the monster atop her, fire or electricity, but it must have hurt. The vrykolak yelped then howled its pain when it didn't relinquish its hold. It pulled its body away slightly and that was enough for Christy to get her arms under her. She pushed up, flinging the werewolf away. It landed on its paws. The other vrykolak had closed rank around them. They planned to let their alpha prove he was above her and then they would each battle to see where she fell among them.

The red wolf attacked but Christy threw up a shield. The werewolf hit the invisible barrier with a crunch. This pack would fall in line as soon as she bested the alpha, proving she had every bit as much right to leadership as Imendand. The problem was she had no idea how to make it happen. She could kill them, but she didn't want to. They had served him well and they might need the pack in the future. With her claim on Imendand's blood, he would never make another. These were all they had, and it looked like they had already lost some. There were not a dozen here.

The werewolf stood on shaky legs and tossed its head around. Christy tried to pinpoint a weakness but couldn't. How had Imendand made them submissive in the first place? He'd taken the strongest men with the blackest hearts and drank from them until they were near dead and then fed them his own on the night of a full moon. How could she put them in their place without killing them? They carried Imendand's blood, the same blood that she carried.

Blood. This was the second time blood was the answer when she was at her most desperate. She just had to find her opening. She jumped over the alpha's back, ripping at the fur of its shoulders on her pass. It spun on her only to find her claw buried in its side. Its momentum did the damage. Its skin was gashed, four parallel rows, and blood ran down its side. They circled each other, the red wolf frothing at the mouth like a rabid dog. It was pissed. It was also giving its body time to heal. Christy didn't let that happen.

She jumped on its back and sank her fangs into its neck. She clamped down, holding on as the monster thrashed beneath her. She did not drink its blood, but rather let it pour from the wound she'd made. Once enough had been spilled, the vrykolak collapsed on the ground. Turning its head and giving her more, not less, access to its vein, signified its surrender. She drew up a mouthful and then stood over the alpha. She made sure the other vrykolak were watching as she spit the blood onto the ground.

One by one the rest of the pack bowed to her, showing her their necks as well. They offered her their weakest spot. They were all bested. She had made her point. She could draw their blood whenever she wanted but she didn't need it. They needed her, not the other way around. She walked around the circle, forcing each member of the pack to lower themselves further. When she was satisfied with their submission, she went to Imendand, who also went down on one knee and offered her his throat. He was her Nephilim; his blood was hers.

As she took a small amount from him, a taste to show the pack she could, a Nephilim and Sinnis whom she'd never seen appeared. They were naked, indicating they had tabalu'd there, and they both had green hair. His was significantly darker, almost a hunter green compared to her emerald color. His entire body was covered in a leaf-rich, vine-like tattoo, while she sported more than one rainbow themed inking. While Christy watched, the Sinnis pricked her finger and let a drop fall onto the ground. Within seconds a plant had sprouted, grown to full size, and blossomed into a multicolored array. The woman plucked the largest flower and a smaller one, handing the second to her Nephilim. With a flick of the wrist, the bloom opened up, and Christy could see they weren't flowers, but a dress and a pair of shorts. The Sinnis had grown clothes for them with her blood.

"Are you the shield maker?" the Sinnis asked Christy, but Christy was feeling a bit woozy and didn't answer right away. Imendand's blood had that effect. "The great mother, Kiyahwe, sent me with a message for the fucking shield maker. Now is that you or ain't it? Relaying messages from the great mother really takes it out of me and I don't want to do this shit again."

Imendand took Christy's hand and pulled her closer to the abrasive new arrivals. "Let me introduce you to Kiyahwe's chosen daughter, Tara Kay, Sinnis to Oren. Tara Kay, I am Imendand Belial Maru and this is my Sinnis, Christy. Before you ask, I know your name because I was there when Kiyahwe sealed the gap in the veil in your orchard and then claimed you with her mark. Tara Kay is the chosen of the mother. Kiyahwe will speak only through her from that day forth."

Kay knew what a big deal it was for a Nephilim to give his full name to another. Imendand was telling Kay that he trusted her. "That's right, but I didn't see you there." The buxom green-haired girl was tiny compared to her Nephilim counterpart, but she held all the attitude. The giant half-breed just stood there and smiled at them.

"I assure you, I was there. I am a shield maker. You only see me now because I allow it." The look in Imendand's eye was clearly pride.

"Why didn't you step up to help when those bastards were trying to come through? Because of you, Kiyahwe had to take corporal form and deal with it Herself," Kay challenged.

"We all do what we will. Choice is an illusion. I did what I was supposed to. We are all Her tools." Imendand said this nonchalantly. Christy wondered if he realized what he said about himself applied to his brother. Belial did what he did, and it was working out. They were all where they should be, with the abilities they needed to deal with the situation.

"How can you say that? They almost came through. Maeve almost died. We could have all died." As soon as she said it, she comprehended. Almost was the key word. If not for this Nephilim's inaction, Kiyahwe would not have shown herself. She would not have bestowed Kay with the birthmark she now wore. The flaming piece of the great mother would not glow from under her skin if not for Imendand.

Imendand saw the recognition and did not defend his choices. He moved on. "I saw you before then too. I was there when those fool witches opened the veil not far from here. I do not know why any would do such a thing purposefully, but they were rewarded by having their powers stripped by the Shinar. If I hadn't been there to close the gap, they would have lost their lives and you with them. Kiyahwe would not have stepped in there. It was not Her plan."

Tara Kay visibly trembled at the memory of that night. She climbed Oren much like a child would climb a tree. Once she was perched in his arms, she said, "You didn't fix that one. It was a Justice Circle. They linked wings and drained the blood-soaked ground."

"They played their part. They powered my work, but it was I who finished the job." Imendand didn't tell them that he had allowed the tear to get so large purposefully, nor that he set it up in her orchard so that the conditions were right for a large hole. He had been trying to draw out Christy at the time, hoping the Daughters would try to use her to seal the gap. If she had appeared, he would have taken her then. As it was, the first time he had let it go on too long and had to use a dangerous amount of his own strength and the lifelines of the Nephilim who made up the Justice Circle. The second time, he had vowed not to let it grow as large but was glad Kiyahwe had stepped in.

"Well, what are you waiting on? They're already lined up for you. Let's get this done so we can go home." Tara Kay was pointedly not looking in the direction of the tear.

"It is not my place. I am not the tool for this repair." He gazed, almost sadly, at Christy.

"Me?" she squeaked.

Imendand shook his head no. "The witches' gap was small, only just opened. What is used to open the tear is what is needed to repair it when the opening is small. I only needed the four types of elemental magic and a gathering of Nephilim. The Shinar have drawn quite a bit of life through here."

Christy touched his arm. "What does it need?"

"It may be time for the One to fulfill the prophesy. Her life is needed to save earth from the Shinar."

Christy saw Samsiel move from his place in the Justice Circle around the gap. She held up her hand to him and he stopped. She made his argument for him, "Genevieve is just a baby. She's supposed to be a Sinnis before her power is called on to save us. This isn't right. I know it's me. I'm supposed to do this, but I don't know how."

Imendand rubbed his face with his hand and then passed it over his bald head. "The veil between this world and that of the Shinar is weakened in the places where human blood has been spilled, innocent human blood of women with power. Once weak enough, it can be cut with a piece of Shinar wielded by a human. It is widened with every bit of life the Shinar are able to pull through that cut." Upset with himself, he shook his head again. He should never have allowed this to grow so much. His drive to claim his Sinnis had been all-encompassing. "This one is much too large to be closed in our way. We would need to add the lifeline of a Shinar to my thread. Even if I knew how to do that, the lifeline would have to collect the exact same amount of plant and animal life that the Shinar took to spread the gap. It is impossible."

One of the vrykolak approached them then. Imendand knew it was not one of his but recognized it, once it had morphed into man, as the one Tara Kay had created in the orchard. His own vrykolak had been setting the stage for a tear in the veil that Imendand had hoped would bring Christy out of hiding when Billy had gotten in the way. His injuries were an accident but the vrykolak responsible had been terminated as a consequence. "I know where to get the lifeline of a Shinar. When I was helping the pack guard the gap, we watched Nathalia fight a half-man, half-Shinar that stepped through. She killed him. Shouldn't the lifelines be gathered in her birthmark? You could use those."

Christy inquired, "Is that what happened to Nathalia? Why is she frozen?"

Imendand answered, "The Shinar use their power to control time and space. If she absorbed even a portion of one Shinar's life, she is in between."

"In between what?" Billy asked, scratching his mop-top.

"In between now and then, here and there. There is nothing we can do. She will either come out of this on her own or she will be trapped."

"Maybe you can do two good things at once. Use some of that to fix the tear and maybe she can snap out of it." Christy was hopeful. Nathalia meant a lot to her.

Before Imendand could tell her that he didn't know how to pull nor manipulate Shinar lifelines, something happened. They could feel the gap come alive behind them. A glowing arm reached through. The Shinar were growing impatient, sensing that their opponents were getting close to a solution. Even without being able to step through fully, the arm was enough to widen the harvesting area around the gap. When the dirt circle began to expand, so did the vrykolak, pushing the gathered people further out of Shinar reach. Christy and Imendand had to do something quick before it was too late and there was nothing to be done.

Tara Kay went stiff. They watched as her eyes unfocused. She slid down her tree-man, who caught her and cradled her limp body for a moment before laying her on the sandy, lifeless dirt. He knelt, obscuring her from the others' view.

"Is she okay?" Christy worried the outstretched arm was doing the Sinnis harm.

Billy, who seemed as comfortable in his nudity as any Nephilim, offered her solace, "She's fine, Christy. It's just a seizure." He explained further when Christy looked perplexed, "Not the floppy kind. It's no big deal, but she doesn't like it when people stare. It used to happen when she smoked too much pot."

"Pot?" Imendand asked.

"Weed, grass, you know, marijuana. But that's not what's happening now. You guys should prepare yourselves. It's about to get epic."

How much more epic could this get? Christy thought. There was a tear in reality and an alien invasion eager to feed on the buffet of life that earth offered. When Kay's eyes opened, she spoke. "We will provide all that is needed." It was clear they were not her words, but Hers and Christy realized what Billy meant. A goddess had spoken.

Tara Kay rested in the dirt. Billy stepped between the prostrate woman and Christy. "Don't look at her. She gets embarrassed after a seizure. It always happens when Kiyahwe speaks through her. Don't worry. She'll be fine."

Kay pushed at his ankles weakly. "We don't have time for my pride." Billy stepped aside and Oren slipped an arm under Kay's legs and the other around her shoulders. He stood, bringing her near limp body with him. She smiled weakly. "Being chosen of the goddess is a bitch."

The green-haired Sinnis pricked her finger on an elongated tooth and squeezed out a drop of blood. As it fell to the earth, Kay gave Kiyahwe's instructions to Christy. Apparently, the seizure resulted from a massive communication from the Goddess, not just the few words She spoke through Kay's mouth. "Kiyahwe says, Yahweh offers a portion of Herself as the thread. It will be pure Yahweh without the protection of Ki to suppress the Shinar nature. It will pull the necessary life from around it. When the plant blossoms, the thread is a match for the gap, and you can use it to stitch up the tear. Do it quickly because the thread won't stop gathering life until you pluck it. It is every bit as dangerous as that fucker's arm over there." She smiled again, less weakly this time. "I took some liberty with that last part. Good luck."

"Wait, you're leaving? What if I mess up and pull it too soon or not soon enough?" Christy panicked.

"I need to get out of here." She gestured to the red teardrop shaped stone glowing below her skin. "Mine isn't like yours or Nathalia's. Mine came from Kiyahwe. It is a piece of Her, and it makes the Shinar crazy to be so close. They see Her as a criminal. She took some of their collective power and made it Her own."

Imendand supported her statement. "When She took form and sealed the gap in Kay's orchard, I saw the frenzy Her proximity caused in the Shinar." He rested his palms on Christy's shoulders. The small touch melted her anxiety.

"It's the reason they are trying so desperately to push through. They want to get to me. You can do this, Christy." Kay smirked. "Kiyahwe says you've already done it," she said, shaking her head, "but Her sense of time is skewed. She's part Shinar." She shrugged and was gone. Oren tabalu'd them a safe distance away. Goddess only knows how far that is, Christy thought.

She didn't have time to ponder Kay's statement about how Christy had done all this before. The vrykolak started growling. The people gathered at the border were disappearing and the werewolves attempted to back them further out of range. "No," she barked at them. "The Shinar aren't taking their prana, the thread is. We can't stop this from happening. It's the only way." It might be the only way, but she couldn't watch as those people died. She turned away.

Imendand wrapped her in his arms and spoke to her quietly. "They came here to give their lives to the Shinar. If these few must forfeit their prana, it is better that it be used to save the rest. Without their sacrifice, humanity will be food for the gods."

He was right. Acknowledging their death was just. Christy turned to watch. The grass of the prairie dried, shriveled, and disappeared. The border stretched until it reached the tree line, then they too lost their green. Leaves browned, crumbling to dust before dropping to the dirt. Branches and trunks crackled and shrunk, leaving menacing skeletons that were easily compromised by the smallest breeze. Erie silence spread as insect and animal life moved to join that of the plants' death. Clothing fell in heaps as the bodies that filled them dissolved. None too slowly, prana was removed from the area and gathered in the plant that grew where nothing else could.

The plant glowed and pulsed. Little more than a bud atop a thin three-foot stem, the plant hurt to look on. When it bloomed, the flower was smaller than Christy's hand, but she knew it was time. She could feel it. The pistol at its center glistened. Elemental magic traveled on the air like pollen and stuck to it. Christy grasped the delicate male flower part and pulled. The thread came easily, and the plant shriveled with the loss. It turned to dust like all of the other flora as Christy approached the gap.

The Nephilim parted to let her through. The Shinar reaction was just as Imendand had described. Christy's presence and that of the thread ignited the Shinar fervor. Their color changed and a blackness grew in their center. It wasn't just a dark spot; it was a black hole. She altered the words of her usual mantra that accompanied her shield making. "We will not allow you to hurt Kiyahwe's children." Christy spoke with more bravado than she actually possessed, but it was soon backed by more power than she'd ever felt.

Christy used the thread as Kiyahwe had instructed to sew the rip in the veil closed, but it wasn't the seam that made the Shinar pull back. It was the song. It came from all around them. It was female, but was accompanied by the earth and Her four elements. Rumbling earthquakes, whistling tornadoes, roaring fire, and raging rivers accented every note. It wasn't just sound. The earth moved under them. It split and they could see the water table's upheaval. The sky was filled with cyclones and flashing lightning. Flames consumed the carcasses of the dead trees. That was what having a bit of untempered Shinar did.

It was done. The sky returned to normal, as did the ground. The tree stumps smoldered, but the fire died. Christy had done it. She'd harnessed the power of Kiyahwe's Shinar nature to protect the world from being consumed. She fell into darkness, felt Imendand's soothing touch and wondered if she, in fulfilling her purpose, was to die.

She smiled in the void of all but Imendand's touch. If this was death, she was fine with dying.

FOURTEEN

Christy woke to find she wasn't in pain, wasn't exhausted as she had been when she formed the gisig for the Daughters. Shouldn't she be after basically saving every living thing on earth? She was glad to be waking at all. Even with her eyes closed, her surroundings were familiar enough to recognize. She was home. She frowned when she realized that Imendand was not in the bed next to her. There was no depression in the mattress that indicated his presence. She missed the weight of his arm or leg thrown over her.

She opened her eyes to find him standing at the window. She took a moment to enjoy the sight of his back. Imendand was in his more monstrous form. Hair covered his beastly large body, not like an animal's fur, but like a macho man. He stood on two legs, but his arms, hanging at his sides, were longer than was humanly proportionate. Of course, that wouldn't be the first hint that he wasn't human, she knew. His wings were massive, hard to miss, and clearly marked him as not fully human. The perfect V shape of his shoulders to hips was what gym junkies strove for but would never achieve. He had muscles where there should be none and that should have made him grotesque, but it didn't.

Even though being without her touch was uncomfortable, he had let her rest. Imendand loved her. Christy had no doubt. She also had no doubt that she returned that love. Imendand was Christy's Nephilim, and she was his Sinnis. That made them perfect for each other. She sighed in satisfaction and he spun around at the sound.

"Finally awake?" he asked.

She would have been disappointed had he changed his appearance for her, but he did not. Christy nodded, never lifting her head from the pillow. "I don't know how final it is, though. I'm still pretty tired." As if to punctuate her point, a yawn stifled her next sentence.

"That may be, but whether you know it or not, you must feed, and I am hungry." The way he said hungry let Christy know he wasn't talking about wanting a soup and salad combo. His eyes flashed red and sent a shiver of need into her pelvis. The tingle in her womb made her acutely aware that she would need to orgasm for him to be properly nourished and vice versa. "I want you."

She licked her lips seductively. "I just realized, I'm starved." Scooting to the edge of the bed on her side, she teased, "How about we give a new meaning to 'breakfast in bed'?" She opened her mouth to demonstrate what she meant, but he needed no demonstration.

Whether he tabalu'd or just moved, he was across the room in the time it took her to blink. He knelt by the bed. In his current larger than human form, that brought his hips to her eye level, his penis bobbing in excitement near her mouth. Save the few stray hairs on the base of his shaft, it was the only hairless part of his body. She explored the smooth, broad, almost purple head with her tongue. She intended to take her time but as soon as his essence hit her taste buds, her plan vanished.

She couldn't think of prolonging the experience. Wrapping her fingers around his shaft, she pumped, hoping to jerk him off quickly. She eagerly devoured his cock, rubbing her tongue over as much surface as possible. Her mind was a blur of hunger, and she had no thought past the silent chanting. "Cum, cum, cum in my mouth" was all she could think.

Imendand let her do what she wanted, knowing he had better control than to finish as quickly as she obviously desired. Big plans for their first coupling since her rise to the rank of humanity's savior had been growing in his head. He traced the curve of her hip and the length of her luxurious legs with the sensitive tips of his wings. Curling one around each of her thin ankles, he heaved her off the bed, showing her how much strength the seemingly thin appendages contained.

She squealed a little but never gave up her oral plaything. He stood, bringing her with him. "Put your hands on the bed," he ordered, knowing almost nothing turned her on more than being told what to do in the bedroom. She was basically doing a handstand on the mattress, only he was holding up her weight. He palmed the back of her inversed head, parting the blonde hair that hung in the opposite direction as usual with his thick fingers. The thought of what he planned to do with those fingers in a minute made him groan.

Hanging by her ankles stretched her body out. She was his captive. He pulled his hips back and fisted her hair to keep her mouth from following its goal when his cock popped free. He traced the features of her face with his penis and then, with a downward rolling motion began to move in and out of her open orifice. The head ran along the length of her tongue before popping past and touching the back of her throat and then trailing the hard roof of her mouth, skating past her teeth, and starting the circuit over. Then he switched to an upward rotation, scraping the underside of his dick along her top teeth and roof before touching her tonsils and pulling out along her warm soft tongue. When he knew she was growing comfortable with the movement he added a little thrust at the back of her mouth and at this angle it forced his cock up into her open throat.

Each time he penetrated, he pushed further, relishing the tightness of that sphincter. Remembering his plans concerning another sphincter, he eased the force with which he fucked her face. He relinquished his hold on her head and ran his hands up her back to palm the firm muscles of her butt. Her skin felt so soft in his palms.

Imendand spread her legs wide so she looked like a human Y. Since he was holding her with his wings, his hands were free to roam. He would never tire of touching her, his Sinnis. Her arousal wafted up and he was sure he'd never smelled a more delectable aroma. Imendand would never tire of how Christy responded to his touch so quickly. Now that she was his equal in power, had surpassed him in ability, he wanted to show her the benefit of being the mate of a Nephilim.

One hand behind, through her legs, he delved into her wet cleft while holding her lips open with the other hand between them. He bent his head and tasted her. Imendand tried to forget that his brother had tasted her first and instead imagined the torture Belial must be enduring to know both how delectable Christy was and that he would never again know the joys of said femininity.

Imendand was not gentle in his devouring of her. He slid his hand from her pussy, gathering her moisture with his fingers and pulling it over her taint to her asshole. He teased the outside of that ring of nerves, while his other hand pushed into her cunt. He stroked her interior G spot while he more slowly eased into her anus. She moaned when he had one finger in. She bucked when he inserted the second. She froze when he took her clitoris into his mouth and, pressing his tongue against it, started drawing intricate designs.

Never before had Christy felt such intense pleasure. Imendand was hitting every one of her spots. She was basically immobilized while he played her body. She could not completely separate the sensations and as her orgasm built, she could not tell where it was originating. It was hard to catch her breath upside down and it was a struggle for the blood gathered in her head to rush to the part of her body that demanded it. She panted and her vision whited out behind the fireworks. The waves made her jerk and spasm in the most unflattering ways, she was certain, but she couldn't bring herself to care. Imendand enjoyed seeing her lose control. When her vision returned, she found herself face down on the bed. It felt nice and she sighed.

"Tell me. Beg me."

Imendand wasn't asking her what she wanted to do. He wanted to hear the depraved desires from her own mouth. If they coincided with his he might indulge her, but only then. Being forced to say them out loud was a twofold aphrodisiac. "Please, Imendand, fuck me in the ass. Push your giant cock roughly into me while I whimper and helplessly squirm under you."

"Show me," he ground out.

Christy lifted her hips off the mattress and parted her knees. "Right here," she said. She planted her face in the pillow and reached behind her and spread her ass cheeks with both hands. "Take me in the naughtiest of places and prove I'm yours to treat how you want."

Imendand placed the head of his cock at her nether hole and pushed gently until it breeched. He took a break once the bulbous mushroom top was in to enjoy the tightness. After he was certain he could contain his excitement and prolong both their pleasure, he applied steady pressure, inching into her. She relaxed, allowing him to bury his cock in her rear end. Even so, she ended up pressed flat again. She could not keep her keister in the air; Imendand was too heavy and pushing too hard. It burned, but she loved it. "Oh, Goddess, yes! Please don't stop." This act was so depraved, and she reveled in so dirty a deed.

He rolled his hips, causing more pressure than friction. "I would not stop, not even if you begged me to. It feels amazing to have you gloriously stretched to accommodate me. Such a tight sweet little ass. All mine." He pulled almost out and then went even deeper than before, stretching her. "You are my good little slut, aren't you, Christy?"

"Yes, I am," she admitted. At that moment, she got it. She didn't revel in the dirty deed. She delighted in being treated and used like a whore by someone who thought of her as a princess. It was the juxtaposition that did it for her, not the depravity. That was why she'd never experienced anything like the joy being with Imendand brought before. No one had ever valued her as he did. It was why she was so unsatisfied with Belial. He had treated her as a delicate princess but thought of her as a whore. Christy immediately wished she hadn't thought of Imendand's brother. "Please, Imendand, harder. Fuck me harder."

Leaning over her, pressing his chest to her back, he whispered in her ear. "Say you want it in both holes at once."

Christy hesitated. She did enjoy that, but she didn't want another man. She wanted only Imendand. "Say it," he growled. He did not enjoy repeating himself.

"I wish you had two cocks so you could fuck me in both holes at once."

Imendand laughed and if she hadn't known better, Christy would have thought it sounded cruel. She had apparently said the magic words. She knew she was about to get it, whatever "it" might be.

Sliding his arms between her body and the mattress, he trapped her arms against her sides and sat back on his heels, lifting her at the same time until she sat on his lap. He never pulled out of her ass. His arm dwarfed her waist. Her breasts rested on his forearm that held her still. He reached down and flicked her clit. She jumped. He moved across the hard nodule of nerves fast. So fast that it went past moving and into vibrating.

Christy bucked and the movement pulled at the cock still buried in her ass. She rocked her hips, enjoying both sensations. "I didn't know you could vibrate. Imendand, that feels so good."

"You forget that I have control over every cell in my body. I can be tall or short, hairy or hairless, monstrous or even feminine. I can do anything that brings pleasure to my Sinnis. I can even have two cocks if that is what you desire." With that, he lifted her up and brought her back down on not one phallus, but two.

They filled her so completely, that Christy suffered a moment of insanity. She laughed and cried as he slid her up and down his lengths, his organic vibrator never pausing. He could give her more than she'd ever dreamed, but she felt confident he'd never give her more than she wanted. Her orgasm took her, and she was glad that Imendand was in control. He kept her moving even as her body tried to rebel. She twitched and yelled, "I love it. Yes! I love you, Imendand." It was like being tossed by the tide. She had no control and rode the waves. Her body was tingling when the contractions stopped.

Imendand pressed her down on his dicks, easing his finger manipulations, and held her still as he came. He let her feel every bit of his ejaculation. He filled her with his prana and then lay them down. They rested, panting. "Tell me what I can give you that no other could."

"Everything; you love me," was all she said, but he understood. The sex was amazing, but no matter what he could do with his body, his perfectly suited love was what he could give her that none other could.

FIFTEEN

"We missed our target," she said as she looked up toward the plateau where the cave opening sat.

"No, we didn't. I want to make sure this is what you want. Belial took advantage of you, fed from you without seeing to your needs, made you think you were his and all of that is on top of his crimes against our bloodline. You do not have to take responsibility for him."

"I know. We've been over this and it's the only solution that makes sense." Not waiting for him to agree, Christy tried to judge the distance to the landing spot they should have made, bent her legs, and jumped. It was the furthest she'd ever made, but it was still nothing. She didn't even have to exert much effort. The laws of nature applied to Nephilim and Sinnis, only differently. She hadn't found any limits so far.

She entered the cave, having felt Imendand land after her. She trusted him to follow, glad she didn't have to be distracted by his beauty. Imagining him behind her was distracting enough, with his perfect chest and ridiculously cut abs both exposed because he wore only jeans. Oh goddess! The way he filled out those jeans was sinful, not to mention the wanton feelings his bare feet and copper skin and wings gave her. Yes, behind her was best. The thought was no sooner in her head than her mind went straight to the gutter. Him behind her *was* best.

"Damn it. Get it together, Christy," she muttered. It was a tactic to break whatever spell thinking about him had cast. She knew no matter how softly she spoke, Imendand could hear, but it wasn't for him that she spoke.

He misunderstood. "This will be nothing for you. You have met every challenge I have given you and exceeded every expectation I had. You sealed a gap that even I could not."

Christy let it go, accepting the compliment the misunderstanding had caused. They reached the tomb room, and she was stunned by Belial's state. It wasn't his position that shocked her, for that hadn't changed. He still knelt before the sarcophagus of his mother, Gazbiyya, his wings tucked tight against his back, his head bowed so deeply that his chin rested on his chest. He looked repentant, but Christy knew that was forced. She had watched as Imendand had increased the pressure inside his brother's trap. Imendand had been so angry he was out of his mind crazy with rage. She'd known he was crushing Belial with heat, but she hadn't realized the extent of that torture.

Belial had been crystallized. From the way he reflected and refracted light, Christy knew he was almost pure diamond.

She looked back at Imendand, but he was unapologetic. In his mind, his brother deserved this. Who was she to judge? She didn't have near the history they had. Not with either of them. She put her focus back on Belial. It was easy to locate the bit of her he had inside. He had consolidated it in his center, protecting it from the change the rest of him had undergone. He knew it was his penance, punishment, and ticket out. He would rather be accountable to Christy than Imendand. It meant he knew his actions merited this.

Belial carried her prana. It was easy to snap the shield around him like a second skin. When Imendand broke the trap he'd set so long ago that had been sprung by Belial's presence, her work was all that stood between Belial and Gazbiyya. The pressure and heat were released, and his body was relieved. It immediately began to heal itself, but the process was slow. He needed to feed, but he'd fed without concern for his supply for long enough. Christy's rules, her control, would take care of that.

His crimes had already been read to him. Imendand had been arresting officer, judge, jury, and jailer but Christy was the warden and the parole officer. "I've given you the only thing you ever really wanted from me. Protection."

"Not only will her shield protect you from those who hunger for your blood, but it also protects you from yourself. Until the time you are claimed by your Sinnis, you are the child of Christy. You will follow her orders and to even think of disobeying will cause you intense pain." Imendand never took his eyes from Belial but tilted his head to indicate he spoke to Christy. "You should speak your rules and imagine them being woven into the fabric of his shield."

"Is that how you do it?" she asked quietly. They hadn't gone over this part and she'd simply assumed that the shield already carried the social barriers she wanted.

Her Nephilim nodded.

She found it quite simple to lay down the law. They were the ones she and Imendand had agreed on and she wasn't tired in the least after she finished.

"Do not forget Gazbiyya," he reminded her.

Christy furrowed her brow. "But there's no reason for him to destroy her body now. He only wanted to cut off the power supply that made him irresistible. What good would it do him?"

"You underestimate his hunger beast. You have me and I, you. You have felt little of the lengths hunger can force us. Until he finds his Sinnis, his hunger beast will ride him, blinding him to everything save relief. There will be times he would consider doing anything to feed. Destroying Gazbiyya would also cut off your power. Yours and mine. He would be free. Free to feed."

She hadn't thought of that. She added that last rule. Belial was healed enough now to move, though he still looked like a diamond. "Come on. We have some apologies to make."

They could have tabalu'd and been there in seconds. Instead they flew, reserving the prana and the strength their extended feeding had bestowed. Belial's wings were too crystalline to fly, so he ran. Christy caught a glimpse of him a few times, but he quickly fell behind. Even superhuman running was no match for the speed at which Imendand could fly. And of course, there was the little matter of the Atlantic Ocean. She wondered what the sailors of the area would think. Would tomorrow's newspapers be filled with stories of UFOs and secret supersonic boats?

Imendand flew them right into the courtyard where a large bunch of children were playing with the adults. Nephilim stood careful watch. They had passed through her shield easily and Christy had taken the time to re-evaluate its strength. It wasn't going anywhere any time soon. Christy knew Imendand was shielding them both from detection because neither a single Nephilim nor Daughter turned their way. The children were another matter. They were oblivious to the fact that Christy and Imendand were virtually invisible to their adult counterparts. Genevieve toddled toward her, Sam never more than an arm's length away. Never would he allow his Sinnis to stumble or fall.

Christy held her arms out and scooped up the girl as soon as she was close enough. Everyone took notice then. Genevieve was the One; they had all sworn to protect her. Anyone who touched her was of great interest to them all. Christy hugged and loved on the girl for a split second before Sam closed in on them. Imendand had dropped his camouflage, and everyone could see them. Sam attacked Imendand viciously and without mercy.

Sword arm met claw.

Christy saw the problem. Imendand had worn his more monstrous form because they were surrounded by Nephilim without Sinnis. Those were the most dangerous, the most affected by his pull. Christy knew he was tired of being mistaken for an Akhkharu. He'd worn that form because it helped him avoid the trouble Belial always had. No one wanted his blood badly enough to risk angering an Akhkharu. Betrayer's blood didn't satiate the hunger beast the way a pure Nephilim's would. Sam reacted without thought. He was only doing his duty to the One.

The Nephilim closed ranks around the children and women. Maeve reached out and tried to pull Christy and Genevieve with her. "Stop! He's one of you." Christy showed the birthright that clearly marked her as a claimed Sinnis. Nothing happened; the fighting continued. She ran toward Imendand and Sam. She was still holding Genevieve. She trusted that the inability to endanger their Sinnis would override the instinct to kill each other.

The two froze, mid-fight, and Christy stepped between them. She stood with her back to Imendand and handed Genevieve to Sam. "See! My Nephilim and I are no danger to the One. He wouldn't hurt her any more than I would."

"He looks like an Akhkharu," one of the women inside the Nephilim circle of protection shouted.

"Looks are deceiving!" Christy turned to Imendand and spoke quietly. "Other people don't understand. Maybe we could save this form for in private. I like you like this. I love you in any form you want to take."

Imendand was momentarily speechless. She had never once reacted with fear or repulsion to his monstrous form. She was not repulsed by what was so effective in keeping others away. She could see him, no matter what shape he might be. His Sinnis was a gift. His hairy beast melted away until he wore his more human form, the copper smooth one. His shield was the same; it made him smell evil. "He looks and seems evil for you! He's trying to keep you at a distance. He doesn't want to tempt you into becoming what you've mistaken him for. My Nephilim is good. He spent his whole life protecting you from yourselves."

"Your Nephilim is Belial and that is *not* Belial. A Sinnis cannot be claimed by two Nephilim," Alisha called out from behind the surrounding Nephilim.

Christy didn't argue even though that was exactly what had happened with Nathalia. It didn't apply; it wouldn't help. "Belial was never my Nephilim. He never claimed to be. He used me, tricked me. He isn't able to shield his pull from the world. He needed me for that and so he let us all think I was his." She took Imendand's hand and brought it to her mouth. She let them all see her drink from the vein in his wrist. No one would drink from an Akhkharu. No Sinnis would drink from other than her Nephilim. She licked her lips clean and tried to keep the intoxicating arousal out of her voice. "This is Imendand Belial Maru. I am his Sinnis. If you want him to go, I will go with him." She stretched up on tiptoes and wrapped her hands around Imendand's neck and waited for him to take off. If he wasn't welcome, she didn't want to be.

"Wait!" Maeve and Camilla came toward her. After a moment of tense silence, Maeve exhaled. "I'm sorry. We didn't understand. Of course you are welcome, both of you." She hugged Christy and the act was like a stick of dynamite in a dam. The women and children poured from behind the Nephilim and flowed toward Christy.

Imendand stood nearby while his Sinnis was welcomed back by the Daughters.

"How is Juliet? Healing okay, I hope. I haven't seen her since the day all this started."

"Juliet is fine," Camilla assured her. The tiny healer was large with child.

"She'll have a scar though, because Jolie wouldn't let us use our blood," Nanae growled from some distance away as he extradited Israel from the bottom of a dog pile. They seemed to have more children than they could wrangle, but also appeared happy in the predicament. Izzy gave the Nephilim a kiss in thanks for his rescue.

Christy enjoyed the peek into family life and hoped she would get to spend some time with those adorable children. They hadn't discussed their living arrangements, but she knew Imendand would let her spend time here if it was what she wanted. "Where's Jolie? I owe her an apology."

"Jolie is spending some time away." Christy must have looked as mortified as she felt because Maeve relinquished her hold on Aaron's hand to pat Christy's arm. "It isn't your fault. She and JD are making some decisions about their lives and what they want for Juliet. They'll come back. You can make your apology when they do."

The desire for her Nephilim was coming off Christy in tidal waves and Maeve quickly pulled back. Aaron took her hand. He was her anchor in this shape. Maeve was getting used to her new life as a Lilitu but the strength of bond between Nephilim and Sinnis easily influenced her. If she wasn't careful, she would have a full-blown shift into Christy's mate's form. Aaron wanted Maeve. Always. He held her to her life as Maeve just as Nanae and Camilla helped Izzy stay Izzy.

Christy knew the second that Belial passed through the Daughters' shield. He ran up but kept his distance from the group. His fear of himself and the pull he had on others was going to be difficult to dispel. The shield he wore as a second skin protected him from tempting those around him, but it would take some time for that to sink in. Everyone stared at him until Christy explained, "You remember Belial."

Belial was still very crystalline but his color was seeping back in. He was inhuman looking, but it wouldn't be long before he was back to his normal golden glowing self. "I must make amends. I wronged Christy, Sinnis of my brother, and caused her place with the Daughters harm. I am sorry for that. Where is the First? I must tell her."

"She is still at the site of the tear in the veil." Maeve's voice was somber.

"Still unmoving?" Imendand asked.

Maeve nodded. "We tried to move her, but she didn't budge."

"Their bodies may be visible but that does not mean they are here and now. Time, space, and reality are all in the realm of Shinar control. I do not know when or where they are, but they will be back when they are needed. The three sisters defeated the Shinar before. I was there. If this child is the One, she will master the realm of the Shinar. She will fold time and space to alter reality and save this world. She has done it already. Ereshkigal accompanied Ishtar and Shaushka," he gestured toward Camilla, "in the great battle of old. Nathalia will wake when she is needed."

More than one person furrowed a brow while trying to untangle his little speech about what will and what has already happened.

Christy smiled. "You can make your apology to her even if she can't hear you, Belial. We'll go there next. Or have we already gone?" she teased Imendand. "But hers wasn't the only one we're here for."

Billy and Minali worked in a section of the garden a little away from the group. Christy could see the tension between them and hoped Belial's apology would help ease it. She watched the three. As Belial approached, Billy stepped between him and Minali and burst into vrykolak form. He was clearly not going to risk what had happened in their apartment over coffee ever happening again. Belial stopped a few feet away. Christy knew he was apologizing for causing trouble between them. He was telling them how selfish it was that he endangered their relationship for a feeding. He was telling Billy that Minali hadn't chosen him over Billy. She was under a spell of sorts and could not help herself. Belial had taken advantage of both of them. He had taken away her ability to consent or not.

Minali's eyes opened wide as she put her hand on her stomach. She swallowed visibly, even from a distance, and said something that did not carry as well. Billy pounced on Belial. The look on his face was ferocious. Christy moved faster than Imendand could have tabalu'd. She pulled Billy off before the fight really got started. Her shield kept Billy from hurting Belial and her control kept Belial from hurting Billy, but nothing could keep Billy's teeth from shattering if he chomped down on Belial's current diamond hard body.

Billy shifted back to human so he could scream at Belial. "You bastard! You follow up apologizing for mentally raping my wife with claiming our daughter as your own."

Christy gawked at Belial. He held up his hands in surrender. "I am sorry, but there is nothing to be done." He tipped his chin toward Minali. "My Sinnis is growing inside her. She calls to me and I can hear her."

"We didn't even know we were pregnant," Minali whispered as she continued to rub her belly.

"He stole that from us too. We can't even find out and celebrate in private like normal people. We have to hear it from this asshole who thinks he's gonna just swoop in and …" Minali's arm on Billy's stopped him.

"We're pregnant." Minali reminded him how glorious this moment should be. Belial may have ruined the surprise, but he couldn't take their joy if they didn't let him. Billy took her in his arms and spun her around shouting that they were having a baby. Minali was laughing when they stopped.

Christy hugged Minali as soon as Billy released her. Minali was the closest thing Christy had ever had to a sister. They both lived with Libby when they were most alone. Libby was their surrogate mother. Now, it wasn't just an emotional bond but a blood one. "If you are pregnant with Belial's Sinnis and I am his brother's, then you and I are from their mother. We're from the same bloodline."

"We're family."

Christy nodded, too overcome. She finally had a place in this world. She had people who not only needed her, but wanted her, loved her. She held her hand out to Imendand, who took it in his own, lacing their fingers.

A slow smile spread across Billy's face and kept going. He was known for his large easy smiles but this one held a vague threat. "I just thought of something. We are going to be Belial's in-laws." Courting his daughter wasn't going to be easy for Belial. Billy was going to make it unnecessarily difficult.

Christy pulled Belial away. "Come on. You hurt Libby and Leonard too. You have more apologies to make. I hope the one with Nathalia goes more smoothly than this one."

EPILOGUE

The Shinar weren't merely filled with life, they *were* life. Nathalia hadn't gathered even half of what the Shinar part had to offer and Nathalia already felt like an atomic bomb. Her birthmark, unable to contain the energy, began dispersing the prana to every cell in her body. Her molecules vibrated on a higher frequency than was natural.

As quickly as it started, it was over. Her body absorbed the power and adjusted to the new higher levels. She smiled at Eiran. She could read the concern in his face and wanted to ease it. *I'm fine. Don't worry. Where is the DakuAhu?*

She waited for his reply but all she got was silence. He closed his eyes. *What's wrong? Are you ill? Were you hit?* Eiran opened his eyes. Very slowly.

Nathalia looked around. The people who stood on the edge of the clearing were eerily still, waiting for their chance to die. The vrykolak, unmoving, guarded the line. Eiran was a statue. It was like the whole world was frozen in time, except for her. She turned to the tear in the veil. The Shinar were there, staring out at her, their rage barely contained. They had lost another portion of their power to this world. She could feel the part of them inside her pulling at everything around her.

This wasn't right. This power wasn't for her. She couldn't contain it. She concentrated on time and imagined a bubble around her. She slowed down the tempo inside her bubble to match the world. She dripped sweat from the effort but was rewarded with Eiran's arms wrapping around her. Not wanting to hurt him, she moved slowly, sensing that she was still not yet on the correct frequency. She laid her head on his shoulder.

When she reached equilibrium, she tried to pop her virtual bubble. Nothing happened. The space inside, around her and Eiran, continued to slow down. The world around sped up until they couldn't make sense of their surroundings. Events were blurred and people were streaks. There was a strobing effect of days and nights passing quicker than seconds.

I can't stop it, Eiran. I've trapped us. What are we going to do? Everyone we know could be dead! The Shinar could be winning and we are stuck...

Eiran knew her mind was attempting to cope with their situation and failing. There was no precedent for dealing with this. "Kiss me."

What? Now is hardly the time for kis...

"Let the world beyond us fall away." Her ability to think, and therefore to speak mind to mind, was obliterated when Eiran pressed his searing lips against hers. If it weren't for that heat, the kiss might have seemed innocent, but then Eiran parted his lips and she tasted heaven.

She thought of the first time he'd held her and how peaceful and perfect it had been even though at the time she had been quite sure she was dying. She had thought that if that had been death, then she welcomed it. From that first moment he had been everything she needed. *I love you, Eiran.*

I love you, too. He spoke silently, not wanting to break the kiss. He knew it was keeping them both sane, blissfully unaware of how fast the world was spinning around them. Her tongue teased. His teeth scraped. Their lips slid across each other's.

Something's wrong.

Eiran tightened his hold on Nathalia. *Mmhumm...*

She pulled away. *Did you hear that?*

He had heard it. A woman was screaming, and she was very close to them. They spun to find the world had stopped or they had caught up with it. Either way, they were in it again.

Maeve lay in a crumpled heap at their feet and Camilla knelt by her side. The healer looked more concerned at Nathalia's sudden movement than the unconscious Abbess.

What happened?

Camilla shrugged but didn't have time for more elaboration. Nathalia crouched when Maeve started to convulse and, when she was close enough, saw that it was not Maeve at all. She wore no corset, and this girl was in her twenties, twenty-two at the most, much too young to be Maeve. She had the same beautiful dark hair as Maeve, but it was short and stylish, and her face was similar enough to be her sister.

Before Nathalia could ask Camilla the identity of the girl, she stopped seizing and started glowing. Flashing was more like it. She throbbed with energy and light. Then Nathalia saw it; the girl wore a birthmark. She was somebody's Sinnis. She looked around for the Nephilim she belonged with but only Sam and Nanae stood in the field with them and Eiran. If Sam was there then this girl was Maeve's daughter, the one who had been a toddler when Nathalia had absorbed the Shinar power and frozen time around her. Two decades she had lost.

Genevieve? she asked.

Camilla nodded. Genevieve's eyes popped open. Then the three fell. Everything around them seemed to stretch, bending the light, making a rainbow that surrounded them. They slid through the multicolored tunnel. Of the three, only Nathalia recognized it. She had fallen through time and space twice before and this one was the same. She didn't know where or when they would end up, but she knew this was big.

The three sisters, Ereshkigal, Ishtar, and Shaushka, were together at last. They were claimed by their respective Nephilim and at full power. There was nothing they couldn't do. If the Shinar shook at the thought of Ishtar being born back into the world, how terrified were they that she was mature and able to absorb their energy with the warrior and the healer at her back.

ACKNOWLEDGMENT

Eric, without you, I would have given up
on this writing thing ages ago.

ABOUT THE AUTHOR

Natalie Gibson writes novels filled with otherworldly violence, sexuality, and the supernatural, and she enjoys mixing horror, magic, fantasy, and romance into her writing. Her stories always have powerful females who change the world, magical creatures that battle their baser natures, and seriously evil bad guys who don't. She resides in central New York with her family.